Star Reacher

By Pamela L. Seay

Pamela L. Seay

Printed in the United States of America

First Printing: May 2018
Pseayauthor, LLC

ISBN-978-0-692-13186-2

For those who dared to reach for the stars.

She stands on the shoulders of others to reach for the stars. When her weight is no longer bearable they walk away, leaving her fallen and further from the life amongst the ones who shine so bright.
©Pamela L. Seay

1

"No!" I almost lost my balance as my right sling-back heel was caught in a large crack in the uneven sidewalk. I slid my foot out of the new fairly comfortable heel to reach down and pull it free.

Thank goodness the cab driver dropped me off on the side of the venue. I was thankful no one could witness me wrestling in a tug-of-war with the pavement for my shoe.

With some effort, I finally freed my gold and silver strapped heel undamaged. I held onto the gated chain fence that contained the tour buses of the bands that myself and thousands of other fans came to see. I slid my numb foot into the shoe and started walking toward the front of the venue.

As a soft-crisp November breeze swept across my exposed back, I breathe in the fresh air. Tonight was going to be magical, I could feel it pulsating through my body. I noticed a uniformed security guard approaching the fence from the inside.

"Do you need help with anything, Miss?"

"No, my shoe just slipped off." I said in my girlish tone

just in case someone important was nearby.

The guard likely in his late-thirties glanced over my body. He stopped his eyes at my breasts that were barely contained in a double-ply shear black tank top. I thought pairing this revealing top with long dark skinny jeans would make my intentions not so obvious. But, that did not seem to work on this security guard.

"So, are you here to meet someone?" The security guard said bluntly, still staring at my small B-cup breasts.

"No. The driver couldn't get through the parking lot. So, he dropped me off here." I nervously tossed my straight bra strap length dark auburn hair. It dawned on me that I was out here alone, at night, on a barely lit sidewalk behind the amphitheater wearing a shear top. I started to panic as I carefully distanced myself from the fence.

Then, I noticed a hooded shadowy figure standing a few feet behind the officer. I could not see his face under the hoodie but I could tell he was staring at me. He was tall, maybe 6'3, and with broad shoulders. His muscular frame was lean. The skinny jeans he wore were so tight, I could see the imprint of his well-endowed manhood.

"I better get in line before it gets too long." I waved to the security guard as I hurried away.

I quickly moved away from the creepy security guard and up the sidewalk.

The front of the venue was a different reality from the dark cold alley I just left. Many fans of the band crowded the sidewalk. Most of them wearing their best emo style with pasty white skin and black hair with bangs swept to the side. It was a sea of black clothing as most of the concert goers wore the 'Death of Love' t-shirts from the band we all came to see.

I made my way to the ticket window to pick up my concert ticket. As I walked to the window a slightly thick girl about 18 years old shoulder shoved me.

"Groupie whore!" She shouted in my face.

I stared back at her unfazed. She was just another insecure emo-goth girl wearing her uniform of pale skin, greasy black hair, and black baggy clothes.

After collecting my ticket from the window, I made my way toward the back of the long, crowded line.

"Hey, you here by yourself? You can cut in front of us." Called out a young guy about 19 years old, with mousy brown hair. He swept his long bangs across his fore head out of his hazel eyes as he smiled at me.

"Yeah, thanks!" I stepped into the line next to him.

He was standing with one other guy and three girls. I noticed how tall he was as his slim figure towered over me.

"What's your name?" He asked shyly, glancing quickly at my breast. I could feel my nipples imprinting through my shear top from the cold air.

"Samantha, but everyone calls me Sam." I reached out my hand. His cold, moist hand clasped mine.

"Josh!"

He introduced me to his friends. The only guy with him was Greg, a slightly overweight pasty 18-year-old. As Josh began introducing me to the three girls, they were already sizing me up.

Lexi was the only one of the three girls who smiled at me. She had dark bronze skin and light brown eyes. Her thick hair that she straightened but started to frizz hung just past her shoulder blades.

Megan was extremely thin and gaunt. She wore no make-up and pulled her greasy blond hair into a low bun. She looked down a lot showing her lack of self-esteem.

"And finally, Nancy!" Josh said her name as if presenting her onto a stage. Nancy was cute but the smirk on her face suggested that she was annoying and likely rude. She had long soft wavy brunette hair, plump olive skin, and dark eyes.

After sizing them up, I realized Lexi was the only one I would likely get along with. The girls quickly turned in towards each other as Nancy whispered to them obviously about my shear top.

With the chill in the air, I began to tremble as I ran my hands over my arms to warm them.

I felt freezing little droplets of water lightly tapping different parts of my body. It was about to rain.

"Great it's about to rain and I don't have an umbrella."

The show was in an amphitheater. So, we would all stand in the rain throughout the performance.

"This will be interesting." Josh whispered in my ear as he stood close behind me. He was becoming more familiar and made it obvious that he liked me.

As the rain fell heavier, a group of people standing behind us pulled out a huge clear tarp. Josh asked if the six of us could stand under and they allowed us to pull the thick plastic tarp over our heads.

Just as the edge of the tarp fell in front of us blocking my view of the long line, a man in his mid-thirties lifted the front of the tarp and peered underneath. He looked directly at me.

"Hey, you want to meet the band?"

Everyone in the amphitheater was drenched from the rain. If my shear top was not revealing before; it was obvious now. The man earlier who invited me to meet the band, gave me and the three girls after show passes. The after show passes were only given to females over 18 years, so Josh and Greg were rightfully upset.

As everyone squeezed through the exit, Josh motioned

towards me. His body stiffened as he inched closer.

"Did you enjoy the show?" He said trying to stall and find a way to keep me from going backstage.

"Let's go! I can't wait to meet Luzar!" Nancy squealed as she bounced up and down. I took this distraction to escape Josh's advances.

I started down the stairs behind the girls toward the stage. As I turned to wave goodbye to Josh, I could see the pain of my rejection on his face. His shoulders slumped downward as I continued down the stairs.

Josh was a nice guy, but meeting Luzar was my reason for being there. Sorry, Josh.

It did not take long for us to make our way to the side of the stage where the venue security instructed the 'chosen' girls to wear the after show stickers on their shirts.

There were seven other girls waiting by the stage with excited expressions. The security guard escorted us through a small door. As I entered the small room, I counted at least 10 other girls already there sitting on two couches on either side of the room. They were not wet like those of us entering, so they must have been here throughout the show.

I walked toward a vanity mirror at the back of the room to try and fix my wet, stringy hair and washed out complexion. Before I made my way to the mirror a door at the rear of the room next to the vanity opened and the band members walked in. They looked over the option of girls available to them as if looking over the meat at a butcher's shop.

Luzar was the last to enter the room. All the girls turned their attention toward him.

His presence was captivating with his tall muscular frame and broad shoulders filling out his tight black jeans and t-shirt. His jet black hair was cut above his ear with a long side bang hanging over one eye.

As he walked past me, he darted a glance directly into my eyes and continued walking. I felt my heart jump to my throat. I tried to stay calm as I stood at the mirror. Breathing deeply to regain my composure, I carefully applied a deep red lipstick and pulled my damp hair into a high bun.

My skin was pasty white from the cold rain. I glanced down to see my tiny dark pink nipples protruding through the shear material of my shirt. The bass player, Johnny, noticed as well. He stared directly at them.

I decided to ignore him and walked back towards the couch at the front of the room. I noticed Lexi sitting on the couch talking to Luzar, who was sitting in an arm chair. I saw a space at the edge of the couch between Lexi and Luzar. I decided to sit down between them and pretend Lexi and I were friends.

"Hey, Lexi. There's a mirror on the back wall if you need to fix yourself up." I wanted to make sure Luzar could hear me. I wanted to distance her from him and make her seem inferior without being obvious.

She had pulled her hair into a bun like mine. But, the rain made her hair so frizzy it stuck out around the edges.

Her dress was wet which caused it to cling to her body that showed her hourglass figure. Even with her makeup completely washed away from the rain, her skin still held its bronzed tone. She actually looked okay, but I wanted to be alone with Luzar.

"I'm okay, but thanks." Lexi meekly replied.

I turned my back to her and positioned my body towards Luzar.

"Hi. I'm Sam." I held out my hand.

"Nice to meet you Sam." He took my hand and held it for an extra second.

"I really enjoyed the performance tonight." I was trying to take over the conversation. Lexi was quiet, so I assumed she did not have much of a personality. It was easy for me to occupy his attention.

"Thanks, Sam. I'm glad you enjoyed the show."

A moment of awkward silence left me searching for something to say to fill the void. Before I could utter a word, Luzar jumped up from the arm chair.

"Is someone smoking in here!" He shouted.

A menacing look flashed across his eyes as he saw the drummer sharing a cigarette with a cute blond girl with large breasts spilling out of her top.

The drummer looked at Luzar and rolled his eyes as he took a long drag of his cigarette.

He tilted his head back and blew a long line of smoke toward the ceiling, taunting Luzar.

Luzar stormed out of the room through the back door the band originally came out of. My heart began to race as I watched my only chance at the rock star life leave the room.

"Do you think he's coming back?" I asked Lexi, worried I missed my chance with him.

"I hope so." Lexi muttered as she stared at the now closed door.

To everyone's surprise, Lexi jumped from the couch and marched to the back door. All the girls on the couch stared at her with both interest and fear as if watching a car crash about to happen.

She opened the door and I saw a young man from the venue's security standing in the doorway. She said something to him then he let her through and closed the door.

Everyone was in shock. She seemed so meek, I never thought she would do something so brave.

My heart pounded in my chest and my breathing shortened. I could not believe she went back there and I was so close. Just as I started losing hope of getting a shot with Luzar, the back door opened and the guy who gave us the after show passes stood in the doorway looking over the room. Then, he looked directly at me.

"Sam!" He called out motioning me to come.

I quickly walked to the door.

"Luzar wants you to come back." He said in a monotone voice.

I was so excited, But, I tried to keep my cool. I saw Lexi grinning and standing next to Luzar.

"Follow us ladies." The monotone man said waving for us to walk closely behind them toward the tour bus.

Little did I know, this was the beginning of the most exciting and heartbreaking year I would ever experience.

2

I wasn't sure what to expect on the tour bus.

As we walked past the tour crew packing and carrying the band's set and instruments onto the back of a small trailer, I saw Luzar's large black tour bus sandwiched between two smaller tour buses that likely belonged to the other band members and opening band.

Luzar's bus expanded on the side to give more room inside. As we moved closer to the tour bus, I calmed a little. I looked over to Lexi and she seemed to calm down as well.

Once we reached the bus's steps, I noticed the first step was higher up. Luzar and his assistant stepped to the side allowing Lexi and I to climb on first. They attempted this as a gentlemanly gesture, but I knew they wanted a close up view of our behinds climbing the steps.

Lexi climbed on first.

She tried to modestly pull down her damp dress as she lifted her leg onto the high step. With the step being so high, we still caught a glimpse of her red thong that barely covered her.

Luzar did not say anything nor did he look away. He continued to stare up Lexi's dress, even as I began climbing the stairs.

As we entered the bus, I was surprised to see several people already there. Even more surprised to see a young boy of about ten years sitting crossed legged on the floor talking excitedly to a middle-aged woman standing in the kitchen area.

In the back to the right were two attractive girls in their early 20's sitting close together at a diner booth style table. Since everyone else on the tour bus ignored them, they were likely groupies invited the same as us except they were not wet.

Two couches were set up on either side of the bus near the entrance. A mix of people occupied the seats except for a small section at the front. Lexi and I quickly sat down and pressed against one another for security in this new environment.

A woman with curly orange-red hair tied into a ponytail marched from the back bedroom past the bunk bed area into the kitchen. She patted the young boy on the head and walked directly to Luzar. She got very close to his face and spoke quietly, but her mouth moved fast suggesting the words were not pleasant. She was average looking with a thin face and frame. She had premature lines around her eyes which were accentuated by her angry expression.

Luzar's shoulders slumped downward as if surrendering authority to her. She pointed towards Lexi and I, then bitched at him some more in front of everyone on the tour bus. The older lady standing in the kitchen area nodded her head, agreeing with the red haired tyrant.

She was not pleased with Luzar inviting two more

groupies onto the bus since two were already sitting in the back corner.

Witnessing this, I began to see Luzar as more human.

I was afraid Lexi and I would be kicked off the tour bus. Luckily, we were able to stay on in the somewhat domestic environment.

After listening to the other onlookers of this uncomfortable scene of Luzar being humiliated, Lexi and I learned that the child was Luzar's son and the red head emasculating him was the mother. Since she was from Atlanta, most of the people on the tour bus were her extended family.

She stormed off and disappeared into the back room. Luzar called Lexi and I to him and extended his arm toward the diner style booth, instructing us to sit across from the other two.

As we set down the girls immediately began sizing us up and we did the same to them.

They were attractive. One had ashy-blond hair in a ponytail and blue eyes. She did not wear a bra but with her small breasts, she didn't really need one.

The other girl was curvier was a luminous complexion. She had huge brown eyes and dark hair cut bluntly at the nape of her neck.

I looked over at Lexi and noticed her dress was now barely damp because of the thin material. My top was nearly dry, but my jeans were still wet and stiff, making it uncomfortable for me to sit. I felt gross, but tried to keep my composure.

While everyone awkwardly looked each other over, I decided to make conversation.

"Hey, I'm Sam!"

They stared at me as if I said something odd.

"Sara." The blond said annoyed as if it was beneath her

to speak to me.

The voluptuous brunette didn't say anything. She just rolled her eyes and kept her attention on Luzar.

Lexi was uncomfortably quiet. She fidgeted slightly as she glanced around the bus trying to find something to occupy her eyes.

"Lexi, where are you from?"

Lexi looked at me with relief.

"I'm from Miami but I've lived in Atlanta since I was four."

Lexi and I exchanged small talk as we waited to see what we were expected to do on the tour bus. Surely, we were not just going to sit there all night.

This was not what I imagined being on the tour bus of one of the hottest rock stars would be like.

I wondered what happened to the wild parties that I read about on blog sites. They all claimed Luzar to be a party animal who has five girls a night!

He walked over with a bottle of wine. His assistant set down wine glasses for each of us and Luzar poured a portion of the wine.

He looked directly at me, singling me out. My heart began to race, and I felt my cheeks warm. The others noticed and looked worried at one another.

"Thanks, Luzar," Sara desperately blurted out as she flicked her tongue on the edge of the wine glass.

"That's nice but the wine is meant to be sipped not licked, like a dog."

Luzar's reply embarrassed Sara as she looked down in shame. I was ecstatic to see him put her down.

The red head came back out from the back and put on a raincoat as the crowd of people at the front said their goodbyes.

Finally, sergeant red head and all these people were

leaving.

As soon as they piled out of the bus, two of the other band members came on.

It was the lead guitar player, Craig, and the bass player, Johnny.

I noticed the lead guitar player was wearing the hoodie and tight jeans like the shadowy figure I saw earlier when my shoe was stuck in the sidewalk.

They gathered at the front of the bus and talked amongst each other in a low voice. Then, Luzar walked toward us.

"Okay, let's play a game."

After two hours of playing card games, truth or dare, and celebrities I'd like to…, we were all relaxed and drunk on wine.

I excused myself to the toilet and Luzar jumped up to guide me.

He grabbed my hand and led me to the back. As we stood in front of the door to the toilet, Luzar shoved my hand down the front of his pants.

Stunned at his aggressive gesture, I did not have time to react before he reached his other arm around the small of my back and pulled me close. He forced my lips open with his tongue and kissed me deeply.

With my hand still down the front of his tight jeans, he pressed his hand on mine guiding it to his crotch. Then, he moved his hand up and down so that my hand stroked his manhood. He moaned and began gyrating his hips.

My bladder tightened as I struggled to hold myself from releasing. I did not want to disturb this intimate moment, so I held it.

"Ooooh, what's going on back here!" The bassist, Johnny, called out.

I used this interruption to pull my hand from Luzar's jeans and bashfully slip into the toilet room, sliding the door shut.

I frantically pulled down my jeans and let out a sigh of relief as my bladder deflated.

I stared at my reflection in the mirror. The color came back to my face and my hair was dry, so I pulled out my hair tie letting the waves fall.

I noticed a trash can to my left full of tissue. I remembered most tour buses cannot flush solids. So, most of the people that were on this bus contributed a urine filled tissue to this trash can.

I added my tissue to the pile.

My jeans were still damp making it difficult to pull them up. I washed my hands and reapplied my red lipstick which smeared from Luzar kissing me.

I slid the door open and walked back into the kitchen area feeling euphoric from Luzar's kiss. I scanned the front of the bus looking for him. To my surprise, Sara was straddling his lap and passionately kissing him.

A sharp pain stabbed at my heart as I watched her grind her pelvis against his. Lexi looked at me with pity as I walked toward her. We sat on the couch across from Luzar and Sara.

Johnny, sitting next to Lexi, looked over at me with his small brown eyes amused at Luzar's performance with Sara on the couch. He searched for my reaction to this betrayal.

Then the lead guitarist, Craig, sat down cautiously next to me holding a glass of wine.

He did not say anything. In fact, the whole night he was awkwardly quiet.

At this point, Luzar had his hands up Sara's shirt as they continued to make out. They seemed to enjoy putting on this show for the rest of us.

I was gone for five minutes and this happened.

The busty brunette set down to the right of Craig. She sat on the edge of the seat so that her cleavage was in his eye line. She had been coming on to him the entire night, but his awkwardness was hard to read whether or not he was interested.

"How's your night going so far?" Craig asked me.

"Okay, I guess." I said feeling insecure.

That was the first time Craig said one word to me all night. He looked into my eyes with a deep, soulful gaze. I felt my skin tingle pleasantly as I stared back into his dark brown eyes.

Craig was very attractive. I did not notice it before because he was always so quiet and not as in-your-face as Luzar.

He was the opposite of Luzar, with kind eyes, tanned skin, and his hair cut so close you could only see the fine blond fuzz.

"Um, so, are you from around here?" I realized Craig was trying to have a conversation with me.

"Yeah, I've been here my whole life."

"You must really like it here." He said sarcastically.

"I must!"

I began to feel more relaxed. I almost forgot about the heartbreaking performance on the couch across from us.

I looked over at Lexi and she was getting very cozy with Johnny. They were snuggled together with Johnny whispering in her ear. She enjoyed the attention as she giggled at him and tugged on his chin-length dark brown hair.

Then, a middle-aged man with a beer gut climbed onto the tour bus. This was clearly the bus driver. Luzar slid Sara from his lap onto the couch and walked to the driver who was starting the engine.

The driver said something to Luzar that made him walk past Sara and stand in the kitchen area. Just then, his son's mother quickly climbed onto the bus with their son in tow. He was obviously tired, with his head resting on her shoulder as she struggled to carry him.

Sara looked horrified as she nervously glanced at the cocky red head. She sat down next to her and glanced at Luzar with a knowing look. Sara slumped down almost sinking into the couch.

Johnny and Craig became very quiet as they watched.

"You guys want to head out with us?" Craig asked me and Lexi.

"Yes." I answered quickly.

I did not want to stay any longer. My pride was damaged, and more drama was brewing on the bus. But, seeing Luzar's behavior was so unexpected. At that moment he did not seem like the masculine, alpha male that he portrayed on stage.

Sara and the busty brunette stayed on the tour bus as we left.

Craig was the last to descend from the stairs. He was carrying a long-sleeved black shirt with the band's album cover on it.

"Here, it's cold out here." He said handing me the shirt.

I was thankful because the night did grow colder.

I pulled the large shirt over my head.

"Do you have a profile on any of the online social sites?" He asked looking down at me.

"Yeah, I'll write down my user name. I already follow you, so you should be able to find me."

I pulled a pen and scrape of paper from my small purse and wrote my username and cell phone number. I handed it to him and he slid it into his back pocket.

"We should head out it's getting really late." I said to Lexi.

It was after one in the morning and the buses were all running, ready to pull out of the parking lot at any moment.

Johnny was trying to convince Lexi to come onto his tour bus.

"You sure you don't want to come. It'll be fun." Johnny said to her seductively, wrapping her arms around his waist.

"No, I have to go."

She gave him a kiss and said goodnight.

"I'll grab you both a cab out front." Craig walked ahead of us to a crew member and instructed him to get us a cab.

He reached into his pocket and pulled out a hundred dollar bill and handed it to me.

"This should be enough to get you home."

I was shocked at this gentlemanly gesture. I thanked him for the money then gave him a hug and kiss on the cheek.

Then, I followed Lexi to the cab.

"Where to ladies?" The driver called out to us as we entered the cab's backseat.

"Where do you live?" Lexi asked me.

"Fayetteville."

"I live in Riverdale. Since I'm closer, he can drop us off there and then I can give you a ride home." Lexi suggested.

"Okay." I was relieved because I did not think a hundred dollars was enough to take us both home.

The cab driver dropped Lexi and I at her home. We climbed into her small silver car and headed to my house.

We talked in the car for the thirty minute drive to my home. I learned that Lexi was 23 years old, still lived with her parents and that she was studying at a local university.

She was shocked when I told her I was 29.

Her shock bothered me. I wasn't that much older than her.

We reached my home and exchanged cell phone numbers. As Lexi pulled out of my gravel driveway, I climbed the stairs of my small Victorian style home and into the house.

"How was the show?" My boyfriend DJ called out from the kitchen.

"It was okay."

3

"You were on his TOUR BUS!!!" Sophie excitedly screeched with her pig nose turned upward on her face. "I should have gone with you! I would have loved to have met him."

I smiled at her knowing that if I'd brought her, there was no way she would have made it backstage.

My boyfriend, DJ, was at work, so I invited Sophie over to tell her about meeting Luzar. Sophie was nice, and I did not have to worry about her trying to upstage me. She was annoying at times though and loud, but she was always a loyal friend to me.

"So, have you heard from Craig?" She asked still excited.

"He messaged me." I said cockily.

"Maybe he'll fly you out to one of their shows." She said staring at me with wide eyes.

"Too bad you didn't get with Luzar. That would have been really awesome. But, you still landed one of the band members."

This stung a bit because my goal was to connect with Luzar. But, I ended up settling for the guitar player. Everyone wanted Luzar, he was like a God. The media was obsessed with him.

You could not turn on the television or look on the internet without seeing his face plastered all over your screen. Even after the tour bus incident with Sara, I still lusted after him.

I thought about Craig and it was exciting receiving messages from him because he was attractive and had a following as well. He was nice and a gentleman to me. I could possibly have a long-term relationship with him. But, Luzar was the star.

After Sophie left, I still could not get the thought of how close I was to actually getting Luzar. If only I did not have to pee right at the moment he and I was kissing.

I logged onto my online profile and went through my messages with Craig. I saw that he sent me a new message.

Craig: Hey, sorry I didn't get back to you earlier. The venue here is mad packed, and we had tons of interviews to do. We'll be back in L.A. in a week. I'd like for you to come out.

I was so excited that he wanted me to come to L.A. There were millions of girls who would have killed to be in my position.

Sam: It's okay, I know you are busy. I'd love to come out to L.A. to see you!

After sending the message, I went onto his profile page and looked through his pictures. I noticed one with him and Luzar sitting on a dark green couch in a low-lit room.

Luzar was sitting confidently with his eyes penetrating

through the picture. It's as if he was looking directly at me.

Craig was sitting with his usual slouched back, shyly looking at the camera.

Luzar definitely outshined Craig. My eyes stared longer at Luzar's image than at Craig's. He had a charisma that seduced you.

I went onto Luzar's profile.

His picture was so captivating with him looking at you with his head tilted downward so that a shadow cast over his eyes and his long bangs hung to one side of his face.

I decided to play their album while I looked through Luzar's photos.

While looking at his photos, I began to sway seductively in my chair. Reminiscing about our encounter on the tour bus, I closed my eyes and leaned my head back.

I ran my fingers over my breasts and felt myself pressing against my panties. I lightly touched the front of myself.

My thighs tensed as a pleasurable sensation rose from between my thighs. It felt so good, my head became light and my mind stood still.

I pressed firmer against myself over the small area. My breath deepened and the heat from the blood rushed to my face making my skin turn red.

My whole body stiffened as I no longer had control. For a moment, my surroundings felt distant, as if I transported to another world.

As I came back to consciousness, I noticed a small wet spot under me in the chair's cushion. I grabbed a towel we used to dust the computer and patted the spot. I could not believe just looking at Luzar's picture made me feel this way.

I saw that I received a private message. I assumed it was from Craig, so I went back to my profile. To my surprise, it was from Luzar. I was in shock. My heart began beating violently as I opened the message.

Luzar: What's up? Will we have a chance to finish what we started on the tour bus?

I cried out.

I had no idea how to respond to his message. I decided I should say something, so I would not offend him.

Sam: I don't know. You may have missed your chance.

What were the odds of Luzar messaging me right as I was going through his profile photos?

I thought there must have been a strong spiritual connection between us. That he was thinking of me as I was thinking of him. Maybe this was a sign he and I were meant to be together.

I decided to call Sophie. I had to tell someone about this.

"What's up, girl!" Sophie picked up after the first ring. She always tried to sound so cool.

"Guess who just messaged me?"

"Was it Craig?"

"No. Luzar!" I whispered excitedly over the phone.

"What?! No way! What did he say? Did you reply?"

I read the messages between Luzar and I.

"Do you think I could have pushed him away with my reply? He did not message me back, but he read my message." I asked Sophie.

"No, girl. You have to keep him on his toes."

As Sophie and I continued our conversation about

Luzar, I heard the front door open. It was my DJ coming in from work.

"Hey, girl. DJ's home. I'll call you tomorrow."

I hung up the phone and closed my profile making sure to clear the browsing history.

"Sam!" DJ called out. "What are you doing?"

"Nothing. I was just talking to Sophie."

4

DJ was once the love of my life.

We had so many plans of pursuing our goals and being successful. But, DJ had no ambition.

He was extremely attractive with his short, spiked black hair and deep dark brown eyes that use to make my knees weak. And, his job as a plumber kept him in really good shape.

He's an amazing song writer. I tried to get him to write with a band that wanted to hire him. But, he never followed through. It was this insecurity that made him unattractive to me. He was sexy, but his lack of confidence in his talent bored me.

We also rarely made love anymore. He tried on several occasions, but I either just let him do all the work or I pretended to not feel well.

I was always relieved when our work schedules were not in sync.

This meant we rarely had off days at the same time. When he was working on a big project, I did not have to worry about seeing him too often.

* * *

I parked my car near the employee's entrance at the mall where I worked as a make-up artist and salesperson at a high-end department store.

I started working here three years ago to network and meet influential people. I have been asked out a lot by very wealthy men. I don't accept because most of them are married.

It was the first week of December and the winter had become colder. I could see the fog from my breath as I rushed into the store.

I walked directly to the employees' locker room making sure to walk confidently with a long stride just in case someone important was watching me.

I hung my cashmere blend coat with matching gloves that I got on sale. I checked my reflection in the full-length mirror and told myself how beautiful I was. I should have been shopping in that store not selling cosmetics.

As I made my way to the makeup counter, I saw Ashley applying lipstick in a mirror. She loved wearing deep red lipstick. It looked good with her pale skin and long black hair.

I always saw her stealing the tester makeup. She got away with it because she was the star seller of the makeup department. But even as the star, she could not afford the high-end brands just like the rest of us.

"Hey, Sammy!" Ashley called out cheerfully flipping her hair.

I hated when she called me Sammy. She always had this condescending way of giving people pet names making them seem inferior to her. I always gave her one of my tight-lipped smiles letting her know I was annoyed. But, she did not care because being annoying was the point.

At work, I did okay. I made enough to live on along with DJ's income. I was in my last year of cosmetology school. So, soon I would be working as an aesthetician in a high-end spa.

Ashley made her way over to me.

"So, I heard you hung out with Luzar on his tour bus." She stood with her arms crossed looking me over and mentally comparing our attractiveness.

"Yeah. It was fun." I had to be cautious about what I shared with Ashley. She was a major gold-digger. We all wanted rich, famous men to sweep us off our feet, but Ashley definitely took it to the next level. She had no shame.

She would lie, spread rumors, steal, and bed the wealthy husbands of the women she sold make-up to. Even with her beauty, every wealthy guy she tried to snare eventually saw right through her and dumped her.

"Are you still talking to Craig from the band?" She was prying me to spill.

Ashley had a knack for getting information. Sophie must have said something to one of her friends. I forgot we knew some of the same people. But, I did not blame Sophie because Ashley was a major manipulator.

"Sometimes." I replied.

"What do you guys talk about?" Now, she was going into full manipulator mode as she closed in on me, now only two inches from my face.

Ashley used this move to intimidate me trying to see if I had something useful.

"Just personal stuff." I turned away from her and pretended to look for something in a bottom cabinet. But, Ashley did not get the hint.

"Personal stuff?" She mocked me, "Oh, you must be

close. Well, he used to talk to a friend of mine. Actually, I think they still talk."

This hit a nerve because I had not heard from Craig in a while. Not since Luzar messaged me. It seemed strange, I thought maybe he knew Luzar messaged me and became upset.

After I spent the day dodging Ashley and putting up with snobby shoppers, I could not wait to get into my warm car and drive home.

As I sat in my car waiting for it to warm up in the cold mall garage, I turned on my radio and went through the stations hoping to hear a song from the band "Death of Love". With the heater blowing on full, my body began to defrost.

I noticed the red light on my phone blinking. It was a text message from Lexi. I had not heard from her since the night of the concert.

Lexi: Hey, Sam! How you doing? It was cool meeting you. Sorry for not texting sooner.

Lexi was really nice.

I did not hang out with many girls except Sophie. I liked Sophie, but she was really annoying and embarrassed me in public when she got drunk.

She seemed like someone I could have as a wing-woman.

Anyway, I had not heard from Craig in a while and I wondered if she was still in contact with Johnny.

5

"They can see who's viewing their profile!"

I called Lexi when I got home and realized DJ was not there.

She informed me that the social site I was on allowed users to see who viewed their profiles, how long they were viewed, and how many times a person viewed their page.

"Lexi, I've been on both of their profile pages, constantly." I confessed.

I would leave the page up for hours, occasionally refreshing it to see if they posted anything new.

No wonder Luzar messaged me when I was looking at his page and fantasizing about him. And, Craig must have known that I was looking at Luzar's profile. No wonder he was ignoring me.

I told Lexi about Luzar messaging me when I was on his page and she informed me that he probably saw that I viewed his profile.

"Well, be careful with Luzar. He's a major player. He tries to get girls to have orgies with him and the other band members." Lexi warned.

"Did Johnny tell you this?"

"Yeah, girl. He said Luzar likes to watch girls hooking up with all the band members. That's why he was all over that girl on the bus. She agreed to have sex with the other guys, but his baby mother came back."

"Is he dating the red head?" I asked Lexi.

"No, but she's trying to find a way to get full custody of their son, so she tries to catch him doing stuff. That's why he was acting weird when she came back on the bus." Lexi explained.

"Wow. Well, Craig has not messaged me back since Luzar contacted me. I don't know what to do." I confessed.

"Well, just give it time. They are busy with the tour. But, stop communicating with Luzar. And, don't go onto his profile page." Lexi instructed.

She was right, but Luzar was so sexy. He even strangely seemed more attractive after hearing about his sexual exploits.

Lexi and I talked on the phone for over an hour. She confessed to wanting to hook up with a R&B singer that was having a concert that weekend.

"I have an extra ticket if you want to come with me. It'll be fun." Lexi used her sing song voice as she tried to convince me to go.

"Who else is playing?" I asked.

"A few R&B artists. Maybe a few rappers. But, the main act is Sha. He is so sexy, girl." Lexi said excitedly.

"Okay, I'll go." I had never gone to a R&B concert before. I thought it would be something new to experience.

Lexi and I waited in line outside the downtown Atlanta venue to see the R&B sensation, Sha.

Although it was extremely cold outside, the women

waiting in line were barely dressed.

Lexi wore a red bodycon mini-dress that hugged her curves and pushed up her cleavage. I wore black skinny jeans and a black long sleeve crop top that made me feel underdressed.

The crowd was a lot different from the crowd I was used to at the rock shows.

Here, there were a lot of scantily clad women which made the competition stiff.

They were all dressed in club wear. No one wore a baggy shirt or pants.

As we made our way into the venue past the crowd. I was expecting a crew member to approach us with after show passes.

No one did to my surprise.

This was weird for me because we looked good. Even with all the women dressed up we were still the top ones there.

We made it to our seats at the front with an amazing view of the stage and the backstage entrance.

Not only could everyone with a backstage pass see us, but the performers could not miss us.

Lexi and I were getting along well together. I felt that I finally met someone I could go to concerts with who was pretty enough to get backstage with me.

It was a relief because Sophie rarely made it backstage with me when we went out to concerts together.

As the two opening acts completed their sets, I was still surprised no one gave us backstage passes.

Everyone stared at us even the opening acts were checking us out.

I could tell Lexi was thinking the same. She had a confused expression as she looked over each guy wearing an all access pass entering the coveted entryway to the backstage area.

During the intermission before the main act, I turned to Lexi.

"It's weird we haven't gotten passes yet." I said to her.

"I know," Lexi responded, "Maybe after Sha's set. R&B artists are a little different from rock musicians."

She was right. Rock performers enjoyed having a personal connection with fans. They usually would sit at the bar and party with their fans.

But these performers tonight seemed to keep the fans at a distance. You rarely caught them without a team of bodyguards, ready to beat down any fan who got too close. Some of the security guards even stood on the stage as the singers performed.

Suddenly, the lights dimmed indicating that Sha was about to begin his performance.

The crowd became excited and restless. The opening instrumentals began to play and all the women in the venue stood to their high-heeled feet waiting for their king to grace them with his presence.

I scanned the crowd and noticed it was about ninety percent women.

I felt the intensity of the sexual urges as the women began posing their bodies to display their assets. And, Lexi and I were no exception.

Then, everyone screamed as he ran onto the stage going right into an upbeat song.

Although I was not a fan of his, I would not turn down a chance to meet him. He was attractive with light brown skin and hazel eyes that slanted slightly upward. His full lips parted as he smiled to reveal perfect pearly white teeth. He had a lot of tattoos on his lean sculpted body which was somewhat a turn-on for me.

While he sang his first ballad, he sauntered to our side

of the stage and was right in front of us.

He lowered his microphone and seemed to stare directly at Lexi.

She noticed him looking at her, so she began to dance sexier.

At the end of Sha's set, we still didn't get an afters how pass.

We noticed a few really young women, barely 18 years old, receiving wrist bands from the venue's crew.

I knew that some artists chose younger women because they were impressionable and easier to manipulate.

And, this definitely was the case here.

While everyone left their seats to exit, a few attractive women stayed behind like us hoping for a chance to meet Sha.

I was sure Lexi would get a pass. Sha could not keep his eyes off her most of his performance. He even performed on our side of the stage most of the set.

"Maybe we should just ask one of the guys wearing the venue shirts for passes?" I suggested.

"Let's try it. It wouldn't hurt to ask." Lexi said as the hope of meeting Sha drained from her eyes.

We walked between the rows to the edge and looked down at the crew carrying the stage gear to the back of the venue.

Two other girls were doing the same so they decided to stand with us.

We spotted a young guy talking to a venue security guy. Lexi waved him over.

"What's up?" He said looking us over.

"Can we get passes backstage?" Lexi asked innocently.

"I don't know if any of the artists are still here. I have to check. But, ya'll may be wasting your time." He disappeared to the back.

Soon after, a woman with the clean-up crew began instructing a few other females trying to get backstage to leave. Wanting to save ourselves from embarrassment, we exited the stands along with the two girls.

As we introduced ourselves we started walking towards the exit of the arena.

One of the girls, Layla, was slim with a light brown complexion. She was wearing a long wavy weave that you could see the tracks from the bad sow-in. Other than that, she was pretty with large brown eyes and full lips.

Her friend, Michele, was slim with dirty-blond hair and one of the few white women here besides me.

We followed a crowd of girls toward the exit when we noticed a crew member open a side door to a staircase.

Layla caught the door and the four of us stood there staring at one another.

"Should we try it?" Layla asked.

"Why not, all they can do is tell us to leave." Lexi exclaimed.

We snuck through the door and made our way down the flight of stairs. Layla opened another door at the bottom of the stairs and it led us backstage.

There were crew members pushing large black cases with silver trim on rollers through the white painted concrete hallway.

They did not pay us any attention.

"Which way do y'all think the dressing rooms are?" I asked as we stood in the hallway trying to figure out where to go.

My adrenaline was pumping. We were sneaking in an off-limits area and any wrong move, we would get kicked out.

"Let's just act like we got lost if anyone asks." Lexi whispered.

"I think we should go to the right." Layla started leading the way.

We walked with our high heels pounding loudly on the smooth concrete floor, echoing down the long, curved hallway. We made our way down the hallway with no one stopping us.

We came to two venue security guards. An older man and a young girl.

"Can we help you ladies?" The older male guard asked sternly.

Layla quickly made up a story.

"We were invited backstage but got separated from the other girls and can't remember where they told us to go."

The older guard was not buying it.

"Well, ya'll can't enter through these doors."

The younger female guard started laughing. She shook her head and pointed behind us.

"Y'all at the wrong end of the hall. All the dressing rooms are at that end." She said amused.

We all uniformly turned around and began walking back to our starting point.

My feet began to hurt from the pounding on the concrete floor. I was sure their feet were hurting as well, but we were determined to have a memorable night.

We finally made it to the other end of the long hallway. Just as we were walking toward the guards at this end, a group of six people surrounding a man walked past us. It was one of the opening performers, Tyler.

He looked us over as he walked by with his entourage.

"Oh my God! Is that Tyler?" Michele froze from the shock of seeing him.

Tyler stopped his entourage and stared at us again this

time he looked directly at Lexi. He waved us to come over and we began walking towards him.

"I want to meet Sha! I'm going to wait here." Layla called out.

We all stopped in our tracks.

She said this loud enough for everyone to hear.

Tyler waved his hand downward as a sign to dismiss us and he continued walking down the hall with his entourage.

"Why did you say that?!" Michele's face blushed with rage.

Michele turned sharply and followed Tyler and his entourage trying to catch up to them.

Lexi and I followed her with Layla reluctantly following behind us, but a security guard blocked us.

"Are these girls with you?" He called in Tyler's direction as they approached an exit door.

Tyler and his entourage paused as he looked at us. He looked at Lexi again.

"That red dress girl!" He sang out and then he exited with his entourage in tow.

The security guard still blocking us directed us to another exit.

"Ladies, you have to exit through the doors behind you. You cannot go past this point." He demanded pointing at a door behind us that led to the employee parking lot behind the venue.

Bummed out, we exited the venue into a cold paved parking lot. It was now after midnight and we had to climb two flights of stairs to get to the bridge.

As we made our way to the top of the staircase, a male voice called out to us.

"Hey, where y'all going?!" A guy in his late 20's called out as he approached us.

"Y'all trying to hang out with Tyler?" He asked us.

"We were trying to meet Sha!" Layla called out.

"Trust me, nobody wants to hang with Sha!" The guy replied with a snarl.

"If y'all want to see Tyler, go to the Ghost Lounge. He's having an after party there." He informed us.

He looked Lexi over, "Girl, you rockin' that red dress."

Everyone was all over Lexi in this red dress. It was getting on my nerves. Even Jayla and Michele seemed annoyed.

"Thanks for letting us know about the afterparty." I said as I grabbed Lexi's hand and quickly walked away from the guy towards the bridge.

Layla and Michele walked close behind. We were in front of the venue's main entrance trying to decide what to do next.

"You guys want to try the Ghost Lounge?" Lexi asked us.

"Yes, I want to hook up with Tyler!" Michele's eyes lit up.

"Layla, I can't believe you made that comment about wanting to see Sha in front of him!" Michele said angrily at Layla.

"He didn't hear me! I was not that loud!" Layla snapped back.

"Everyone heard you, Layla!" Michele began to blush again, "We could have been on the bus partying with him right now if it wasn't for you."

Michele was right, Layla did ruin the moment for Michele.

"Hey, let's try the Ghost Lounge and see if we can get a second chance." Lexi said trying to diffuse a fight between Michele and Layla, "And, Sha is close with Tyler so there's a chance Sha may be there."

"I'll get us a rideshare to the venue." I pulled out my cellphone put in the location information to request the ride. Then, we waited on the sidewalk in front of the venue.

The driver dropped us off in front of the Ghost Lounge and we quickly got in the line to enter the club.

After being patted down and having our purses searched we approached a man standing at a podium by the entrance door requesting $40 per person for entry. Lexi and I pulled out our credit cards to pay.

"There's an ATM just inside the door." He said without looking up from his cash box.

We went to the ATM as instructed and stood behind a man withdrawing cash.

I noticed Layla and Michele whispering to each other with a concerned expression.

"We don't have any cash." Layla whispered to Lexi and me.

"Can you use the ATM?" I asked her in disbelief they came here without any money.

"We don't have our wallets." Layla said glaring at Michele.

I already paid for the driver, I was not going to pay an extra $80 for these girls to get into the club. Lexi gave me a knowing look indicating she was thinking the same.

Michele looked behind her checking for the bouncer. Then, she grabbed our wrists and made a run for it into the small crowded club.

I could not believe what was happening.

Lexi's eyes were wide with fear as she looked at me.

"Hey, ladies!" I saw the bouncer rushing right behind us.

He managed to get in front of us and spread out his

arms blocking our path.

"Let's go ladies!" He yelled as he escorted us to the exit.

I was mortified.

I'd never been kicked out of a nightclub before.

Everyone watched us as the bouncer directed us out the door.

"This is too embarrassing." Lexi held her hand up trying to shield her face.

"Well, so much for our fun night!" I said angry at the embarrassment of being escorted out of the club.

Layla and Michele really upset me with their immaturity. They did not have a penny between them. I did not have a lot of money, but at least I knew to be prepared and saved money for tonight's event.

"I'm calling my aunt to pick us up!" Layla called out as she pulled out her phone.

"These dumb, broke bitches." Lexi whispered into my ear. Lexi was fed-up and just as embarrassed as I was.

Lexi and I decided to wait with Layla and Michele to make sure they had a way home since they did not have any money to pay for a ride share.

A large blue van pulled up in front of us in the parking lot. It was Layla's aunt. She talked to Layla and gave them $40 each to get into the club. But, I was not sure if the bouncer would let us back in.

We went back to the line outside the entrance and the door guy still not looking up from his cash box took our money and let us back in.

The club was so crowded we were barely able to make our way to the bar. I noticed no one was dancing. Everyone just stood around.

The club was small and dark, only lit by neon blue lights. Most of the lights were over the DJ area which was elevated from the main floor.

Tyler was standing in front of the DJ booth wearing shades and surrounded by ten women in short bodycon dresses sitting on long couches as if in a haram.

The men in his entourage stood around the girls and stared out at the crowd.

We stopped at the bar and Lexi bought us a round of drinks. We made our way through the crowd of women. We were at the front of the stage trying to figure out what to do next.

Tyler stood like a king presiding over his subjects.

All the rejected women crowded at the front of the stage and stared up at him.

Some of them danced seductively obviously trying to catch his attention.

"Do you think we can get into the VIP area with Tyler?" Michele said.

"We can ask someone in his entourage." Lexi said shrugging her shoulders upward.

"Well, I didn't come here to just stand around." I was getting impatient, "I'll ask this guy."

I walked up to the stage and tapped a large man dressed in black with a long beard on the arm. He looked down at me and glanced at my friends.

"Can we come up there?" I asked.

He laughed and tilted his head upward, shaking it as to say no in a dismissive way.

The rudeness was a shock, but I surprisingly was not hurt by it. Maybe because I was not a big fan of Tyler.

The four of us went back through the crowd of women and took our place along with the other rejected subjects.

"Well, I don't want to just stand here." Lexi said as she grew impatient. She didn't seem to be much of a fan of Tyler either.

"We can try going that way." Layla pointed to the far

right of the stage with an opening to a seated area near the DJ booth.

"I don't know if I want to try again." I said feeling discouraged.

"Well, we're here. It won't hurt to try." Lexi led the way to the opening at the side of the stage.

"Ya'll trying to go up there?" a man called out to us.

"Yeah, can we go up there?" Lexi pointed at the opening.

"Sure." The man said moving to clear our path.

We climbed the small step to the seated area occupied by more seductively dressed women.

A man with long braids and a zombie expression, pushed his way past us almost knocking Lexi over. He was carrying a black duffle bag with a large plastic container that did not fit so the zipper could not close all the way. There was a clear liquid swishing it the large plastic container and a label that looked like a prescription.

Lexi and I looked at each other realizing it was a prescription drug used to make an illegal drink.

After the man with the zombie expression made his way to the DJ booth, another man blocked us from walking further into the VIP area.

"No more bitches!" The man yelled waving his hands in front of him.

"We're at full capacity! Get out!" He continued to yell in Lexi's face.

Lexi looked mortified as this man yelled in her face in front of everyone.

"You don't have to yell!" I screamed back at him trying to defend her.

"I don't give a FUCK!" The guy yelled over Lexi's head at me.

"That's it! I'm leaving this place!" Lexi said as she and I

squeezed past Layla and Michele.

As Lexi walked past the man that let us into the VIP area, he reached out and grabbed Lexi's behind.

"Hey!" Lexi screamed as she slapped his hand away.

"OK! Let's go!" I grabbed Lexi's hand.

"We're gonna stay here! There's a guy that told Michele he knew Tyler and can get us in the after, after party!" Layla said excitedly with Michele bouncing happily.

"Good luck girls!" I called out to them sarcastically.

Lexi and I pushed our way through the sea of desperate women to the exit. We shoved open the heavy door and stepped outside into the cold night. It was 4:30 in the morning and I just wanted to go home.

6

"I will never do that again!"

It was the next day and I called Lexi to check on her since she didn't get to meet Sha.

"I understand Sam. That was so humiliating."

I was sitting on a daybed I recently bought for the second bedroom.

DJ and I were not getting along, so I was sleeping in here for a few nights.

"How are things with DJ?" Lexi asked trying to change the subject.

"He and I had a big argument about me staying out so late last night. We have been arguing a lot lately." I confessed.

"Will you try to work it out with him?"

"I've tried talking to him. But, we just end up arguing. I feel there's no point in trying anymore." It was exhausting just thinking about all the arguments we had.

"You have to do what's best for you Sam." Lexi encouraged.

"You're right. I have to get off the phone and study for

my cosmetology exam next week." I lied. I really wanted to stalk Luzar and Craig's social profiles.

"Okay. Call me later." Lexi hung up.

Since learning about the site tracking anyone who looked on another person's profile, I created a fake page to spy on Luzar and Craig.

I still had not heard anything from Craig. And, it hurt that he was ignoring me.

I heard DJ come into the house and go into the bedroom.

He hadn't tried to talk to me since our argument. I was okay with that since I spent most of my time in this second bedroom anyway. It was the only place in the house I could escape.

Whenever I heard DJ's truck pull in over the gravel driveway, my heart always jumped in fear of him catching me looking at Luzar's or Craig's profile.

I could not remember when we became so distant.

We had known each other since high school and lived together for a few years.

But, one day we were making love and the next I could not wait for him to finish and get off me.

Maybe it was a combination of issues we experienced over time.

When we bought this house, it was in really bad shape. There were rodents and defecation all over.

Thieves gutted the place with wires missing from the walls.

The copper plumbing was cut from under the house and even most of the hardwood floors were ripped out.

DJ's credit was so bad he could not get a mortgage loan, so I had to co-sign for the house.

I cried every night because I felt trapped here. After a year and a ton of our savings, DJ worked his magic and made this place a beautiful home. But, by that time our relationship went through a lot.

DJ was an amazing song writer and musician. He created the most beautiful songs. A lot of the music we played in the house he created. I tried to get him to give the songs to a producer, but he said he was not ready.

He always blew me off when I suggested he publish his music. He was afraid of being judged or rejected. And, it was this weakness that really turned me off from him.

I wanted someone who put themselves out there. Who did not care what others thought. Maybe that was why I was so attracted to Luzar.

He was completely himself. He put himself out there for the world to criticize and he did not care.

I really wanted Luzar. But, I felt bad that I did not feel the same about Craig.

Why could I not be with the one I wanted? Why did I have to stick with Craig or DJ when my heart wanted Luzar?

DJ left to hang at the local bar with some of his friends. I was relieved when he left and decided to watch television and relax on the couch in the living room.

My cell phone rang, and it was Sophie.

"Hey, girl! Just checking on you. Have you heard from Craig or Luzar, yet?" Sophie asked.

Wow, Sophie really jumped right into the gossip.

"No. I'm not sure I ever will at this point." I felt worse now at the thought of my chance being gone.

As I started feeling depressed a 'Death of Love' video came on the television.

"Sophie, their music video just came on." I said shocked.

"That can't be a coincidence!" Sophie replied.

"What if this is a sign that you're meant to be with him?"

"I don't know. But, this is so weird that I feel they will never contact me and their video comes on." I said hopefully.

"Maybe you should look into this." Sophie suggested, "There's a girl at my job who goes to these psychic fairs every month. She said they predicted her marriage, job, and even when she would meet her husband!"

"What? Are you serious?"

"These psychics are the real deal. They may be able to help you." She added.

"I don't know, Sophie. A psychic!" I was skeptical.

"It's worth a shot. You never know." Sophie said trying to convince me.

I decided to give it a chance. What's the worst that could happen?

Standing outside in a line of about fifty people, the psychics were in a large grey trailer that sat in an empty parking lot on Roswell Road.

I stuck out like a sore thumb here. The line was full of people wearing bomber jackets and flannel trying to keep warm.

They all looked desperate and spoke about their readings with childlike excitement. I was wary of spending twenty dollars for a fifteen minute reading, but I allowed Sophie to convince me to come.

A list to designate the psychic you wanted a reading from was past down the long line. When it reached me and Sophie, she wrote down two psychics' names.

"You want Spring or Ezda. I normally do both." Sophie advised.

"I'll just have a reading with Spring." I did not want to spend $40 on psychic readings.

"She's the best one. Everyone tries to get in to see her."

Sophie said.

After about an hour and a half of waiting outside, Sophie already had her reading with Ezda and was waiting with me for the reading with Spring. If I had not already paid my twenty dollars, I would have left an hour and fifteen minutes ago. I could not believe I let Sophie talk me into sitting here this long.

"Sophie!" The coordinator holding a clipboard with our names called out.

"I'm here!" Sophie jumped up excitedly rushing to the back of the trailer.

Finally, I was next.

Sophie returned after her psychic reading with a grin on her face. She inhaled and exhaled meditatively and sat down next to me. Before I could inquire about her experience the coordinator with the clipboard called my name.

He pointed me in the direction of a lady with a brown complexion and wearing a curly wig.

She was sitting at a table with crystals of different colors laid out in front of her. She stared directly at me with her expressive large dark-brown eyes.

"Hello, my name is Spring. Welcome." She extended her hand to greet me.

"Sam." I said shanking her hand and sitting in the chair across from her.

"Is there any area you want to focus on today?" She asked.

"I guess my romantic and financial future." I was not sure what to ask for. This was all so new to me.

Spring closed her eyes and laid her hands flat on the table between the crystals. She inhaled deeply, then held her breath for a few seconds and slowly breathed out. With her eyes still closed, she tilted her head as if someone was whispering in her ear.

I began to question if she was acting. Just as I started to feel uncomfortable, she opened her eyes and looked at me in a tranced expression.

"I see you being pulled between three men. One you live with, one who likes you, but you are hesitant, and the third is the one you want but he has women all around him." Spring closed her eyes again.

She was correct, but I thought to myself that Sophie could have told her this.

She opened her eyes again with the same tranced expression.

"The one that you want, I see him as a leader of something. He's admired by many and women are available to him. I see that he is interested in you, but he is very careful. He will play games with you to see how you react."

She went back into her meditative state. She opened her eyes again, still tranced.

"The man you live with. He is holding you back from reaching your full potential because he is afraid he is not good enough. He will not do well in the future, especially financially. His financial setback will affect you, but you will work it out and be okay."

She stopped again to listen to the invisible voice as she tilted her head.

"The second guy will make another attempt to be with you. You have the right to choose who you want to be with, but I see him as being the better one for you. But, he will not wait for you to choose. My suggestion is to just be their friend and wait because your feelings are likely to change."

At this point, I was freaking out inside. She was accurate, but I still held on to a bit of my skepticism.

"I do see you are considering being on your own." Spring continued, "I also see a female presence around you. Someone new that will be like a sister type. Her appearance is the opposite of yours. She will be essential to you moving forward with your choice. She may even know someone close to them."

"Wow! Yeah, I think I know who you are referring to. I met a girl at the same time I met them. She talks to one of their friends." I could not believe she was seeing all of this.

"Well, you and she will become close. But, be careful with her." Spring warned, "She is nice, but she will leave you behind and look out for her own interests. You have to make sure to meet whomever she can introduce you to and develop your own relationships."

I stared back at her in disbelief.

"We have three minutes left. Is there anything else you want to look further into?" Spring asked.

"Yes. I have not heard from either of the guys in a while. Should I contact them?" I asked realizing this is what I really needed guidance on.

"You should. Just remember to take your time and be their friend." Spring advised.

This was exactly the confirmation I needed to move forward in my quest to getting what I wanted. I could not wait to tell Sophie.

7

"This place looks decent." Sophie said looking at an online apartment listing with an unsure expression on her face.

I wanted to move into the city; preferably East Atlanta. That was where most of the hip, rocker types lived. But, most of the somewhat decent apartments were extremely out of my price range.

The only place that was slightly livable within my budget was in an old guy's basement with one tiny window towards the ceiling.

"If you have a roommate you can get a better deal on an apartment." Sophie suggested, "I would room with you, but I bought a house in Milton."

Honestly, I would not share an apartment with Sophie ever again. We were at each other's throats the last time we shared a place.

"Yeah, I was thinking of asking Lexi. But, I don't know her that well." I said to Sophie.

"I need to meet her." Sophie demanded, but I ignored her.

There was no purpose for her to meet Lexi. But, I did

want to keep Lexi close since she was still in touch with the bassist from the band.

Lexi still lived with her parents, so it was likely I could convince her to become my roommate. But, mostly, I needed to keep a connection with the band. The psychic said she was important in me reaching my goals so maybe it was meant for us to live together.

"This is the best area to live in." I explained to Lexi as I drove us to an apartment building in midtown on Ponce de Leon Avenue.

"Between East Atlanta and Midtown is where all the famous musicians hang out when they come here." I studied all the popular musician's social profiles and fan pages to see where they hung out when in Atlanta.

I was trying to convince her to move with me into the city.

Also, I saw on Craig's social profile the band was coming here to mix their upcoming album. I knew Johnny would want to see her, so this was my way to get another shot at either Craig or Luzar.

"This one is the least expensive, but it is nice and in the perfect location." I watched Lexi nodding her head while looking out the window at the large brick building.

Lexi was quiet most of the drive. She mostly stared out the window.

We had an appointment to look at one of the units in the old converted warehouse. It looked run down on the outside but the pictures online of the inside were acceptable. With Lexi and I splitting the $900 rent, this was all we could afford.

The leasing agent showed us around the two bedroom/ two bath, first floor apartment. It was larger than I thought with each bedroom separated by the living room.

This was perfect!

The unit had concrete floors that were painted black and white walls with really high ceilings. The energy here felt good. I knew this was the place to start my new life.

After viewing the apartment, we decided to take it. The only issue was Lexi did not have a job because she was a full-time student, so I helped her get a position at the department store I worked at. The manager loved me, so she was hired right away.

Everything was falling into place.

This was the first step to getting everything that I wanted. I imagined myself living in Los Angeles in a huge mansion, shopping, and hanging out with my new famous friends. I just needed Lexi to play her part and get me back in with the band.

"So, have you heard from Johnny?" I did not waste time grilling Lexi for information on the band members.

"I spoke to Johnny and he said within a few months they would be here for a week in the Spring to mix their new album." Lexi revealed.

"That's awesome! You have to invite me to hang out with them."

"Of course. We're roommates, now!"

8

The winter months went by quickly, and it was now early March and Spring was just around the corner.

Lexi and I were doing very well living together.

She was a great employee at the department store and paid the bills on time. We hung out and partied together. Everything flowed easily.

I still had not heard from Craig nor Luzar. They liked a few of my pictures on my profile. I made sure to include Lexi in my pictures since she still spoke with Johnny. But, I wanted more than likes on my pictures. I wanted to be a significant part of their life.

With the band coming to Atlanta soon, I continued to pump Lexi for updates. I needed everything to go as planned.

"Have you heard from Johnny?" I asked her. I needed to be sure that he was planning to see her when he came.

"Yeah. He texted me yesterday." Lexi was not as forthcoming with information about them lately.

"You didn't tell me that! What did he say!" I pushed her to give me more details.

"They'll be here next week." She rolled her eyes at me.

"Well, give me details. What did he tell you exactly?" I had a feeling she was keeping something from me.

"He didn't go into detail. He just said they would be here Friday next week." She was becoming annoyed with my pushiness. I did not care, the only reason she was my roommate was to make sure I got close to the band.

I remembered what the psychic, Spring, said about getting what I needed from Lexi because she could end up with the life that I wanted.

I could not wait for the following week to go by.

When Friday finally came, I made sure to stay close to Lexi all day.

Every time she checked her phone, I asked her if it was Johnny. Each time she said no, and she even tried to hide from me at work. But, I found her hiding in one of the dressing rooms with her phone.

"Is that Johnny?" I asked.

Lexi rolled her eyes at me, "No."

"You should call him!" I said sternly as she sat on a low stool.

"He will call when they are here!" Lexi yelled at me.

I was taken aback. She never snapped at me like this.

I left her alone for the remainder of the day at work.

After I finished my shift, I went to a salon to have my hair professionally blown-out. I needed to look perfect for tonight.

I arrived at our apartment and spent an hour doing my makeup.

At 6:00 pm, Lexi came to my room, "They're here!"

This was it! This was really happening!

We drove in Lexi's car into Downtown Atlanta to the

band's hotel. My stomach fluttered with excitement as Lexi pulled her car into the valet.

We took the elevator to Johnny's suite.

He opened the door promptly after Lexi knocked as if he was waiting at the door.

"Hey!" He pulled her to him giving her a hug.

"Hey, Sam." He said reaching out one arm to give me a half hug to be polite.

"We're meeting the guys at the rooftop bar." He said to Lexi.

We left his room and piled into the elevator. Johnny swiped his room card on the reader for the roof.

Once we were out of the elevator, I scanned the large area for Luzar.

The rooftop lounge was lit by several strings of small light bulbs. There were five beds with shear drapes attached to the posts for privacy. The area was larger than I expected with a small dance floor between the beds and the main bar.

On the other side of the bar were several high tables with chairs that were occupied by a crowd of people.

As we settled onto the high stools at the bar, I noticed Johnny talking to the drummer, Zach. I did not realize how short he was. He was shorter than me by almost two inches.

Zach looked me up and down as if checking me over and nodded his head in approval.

He walked to me and introduced himself.

"Hey, I'm Zach." He held out his hand and smiled with a crooked grin.

I never noticed him in the band. He was not unattractive. He had dark hair and tan skin.

"Sam." I shook his hand

I looked over at Lexi and she was laughing at

something Johnny was whispering to her.

Zach scanned his eyes over my body. I wanted to get away from him, but I could not find an excuse to remove myself.

"You are absolutely beautiful." Zach said still holding his creepy stare.

"Thank you." I tried to stay calm and avoid his eyes. I did not want to give him any indication of interest.

Then, out the corner of my eye, I saw Luzar and Craig walk up to Johnny at the bar. They recognized Lexi and said hello. Then, they glanced at me but tried to avoid making eye contact.

I felt a weight in my heart. They sat at the bar next to Johnny and just talked to each other. Johnny focused all his attention on Lexi and I was stuck with creepy Zach.

Well, at least Lexi was enjoying herself.

After an hour, I allowed Zach to flirt with me so I would not feel awkward sitting alone.

I wanted to cry. This night was not supposed to go this way.

"Well, I'm gonna call it a night guys." Luzar called out.

"Let's head back to my suite." Johnny said grabbing Lexi's hand and pulling her to her feet.

I watched in horror as Luzar and Craig stood up to leave the bar.

"So, you want to hang out?" Zach said to me in a low sexy voice.

"Nah, I'm gonna head back home with Lexi."

When I said this, Zach and Johnny gave each other a knowing look. Johnny looked at me bewildered that I suggested Lexi was leaving with me.

We all piled into the elevator and I positioned myself to ensure I was in Luzar's eyesight. He glanced at me then started talking to Craig again. Craig did not look at me. He behaved as it I was not there.

We reached Johnny's floor first.

As he and Lexi exited the elevator, I turned to say goodnight. But, before I could utter a word, Luzar put his hand on my lower back and pushed me out of the elevator.

I was mortified.

Luzar pushed me from the elevator as if I was an annoying fan girl. I tried my best not to cry.

Johnny and Lexi were so involved in each other, they didn't even notice my humiliation.

I followed them into Johnny's suite and the three of us stood in his living room area.

"So, you staying the night?" Johnny said to Lexi.

I could not let her stay here. The night did not go the way I expected, and I was not going to leave alone.

"No! She has to drive me back home." I blurted out at Johnny.

"Well, can you drive her car home?" Johnny snapped at me.

"I'm not leaving her here." I shot back at him.

Lexi stood there with her eyes wide with disbelief at Johnny and I arguing.

"Well, you can come with us if you want." Lexi suggested to Johnny.

"Okay. Let me grab a few things." Johnny said walking into the bedroom.

I could not argue with him coming over. I didn't expect her to suggest it. I especially didn't expect him to agree.

They talked the whole 10-minute ride to our apartment. Lexi didn't seem to care that my night did not go well.

At our apartment, she showed Johnny around. Then, they went into her bedroom and shut the door.

I knew she was going to be intimate with him. So, I went into my bedroom and shut my door as well. Then, I washed off my makeup, climbed into bed, and cried myself to sleep.

9

I awoke the next morning feeling as if I'd ran a marathon in my sleep.

My eyes were red and puffy from crying all night.

I didn't want to run into Lexi and Johnny, so I put on my workout clothes and left for the gym before they got up.

Lexi's door was still closed so I assumed they were still sleeping. Then, I heard Johnny moaning as I was leaving the apartment. It really irritated me to hear them having sex.

I let the front door slam shut, marched to my car, and sped off towards the gym.

In the gym's parking lot, I sat in my car for a while.

It felt as if I was in a dream world. But, this dream was more of a nightmare. I had to figure out my next move.

Sophie sent a text message asking about last night. I was too embarrassed to call her.

I wanted to cry again as I replayed last night in my head.

My cell phone rang, and it was Sophie. I knew she

would not stop calling until I answered.

"Hey." My voice cracked.

"Girl! What happened last night? Did you hook up with Luzar?"

After telling Sophie every detail of last night, she was shocked at Luzar's reaction to me.

"Well, it's not like you slept with any of them like that slut, Lexi." Sophie said angrily, "Those are the type of girls they like. I can't believe she ignored you like that."

"She didn't even care. She was just concerned about herself." I added.

"You still have your dignity, Sam. But, you need to get Lexi out of the picture and go after what you want."

She was right. I could not sit here and accept this fate.

"I think I have a way to get Lexi out of my way."

I went into work with a plan later that day. Lexi's supervisor in the men's fashion department at work really liked me. So, I decided to use him to get Lexi out my way.

"Phil, how are you?" I called out as I spotted him at the register.

Phil was in his mid-forties and balding. He always flirted with me at work even though he was married. I knew he would do anything I asked of him.

He looked so excited to see me approach him.

"Hey, beautiful. What do I owe the pleasure?" He looked at me with his awkward sultry expression.

"I need a favor to ask." I said.

"What's up? Anything for you princess."

"Lexi's been getting in my way at our apartment. Tomorrow night I have something important to do. Is there any way you can put her on the schedule? It would mean a lot to me." I used my pouty expression. He always fell for this look.

"Don't worry. Lexi will not be bothering you tomorrow night." He said as he winked at me.

"I was supposed to be off tomorrow night!" Lexi yelled as she stomped into the break room at work.

Phil came through for me.

"What happened?" I asked trying to act surprised.

"Phil put me on the schedule for tomorrow night. I was supposed to be off." Lexi complained.

"I have to text Johnny that I won't be able to hang out tomorrow night." She said pulling out her cell phone and typing a message.

"What's happening tomorrow night?"

"Johnny wanted to take me out on a date." She said as she continued typing a message on her cell phone.

"Well, I'm sure you will see him after work."

Lexi ignored me, obviously reading a reply from Johnny.

"What did he say?" I asked, shocked that he text her back so quickly.

She didn't hear me as she stormed out of the room.

I was ecstatic. While she worked tomorrow night, I could hang out with the band. I just needed to find a way to get invited back to the hotel.

I left work early that day and raced to the apartment.

I called Sophie to get her opinion on what I should do next.

"Send a friend request to Zach. Then, wait until tomorrow and message Zach that you and a friend are coming to the hotel bar. He's a horny dog, so he'll take the bait. Then, just pray that Luzar shows up." Sophie was a mastermind at this.

I sent a friend request to Zach and he accepted immediately. I felt hopeful again at my chance to get

Zach. She immediately started asking Zach random questions so that I could make my move on Luzar.

"Hey, Johnny!" I hugged Johnny. I decided to use him as a way to interject myself.

"What's up, is Lexi with you?" He asked with his eyes searching behind me.

"No. She had to work." I said annoyed.

I moved in on Luzar. I had to push past two of the girls to get face-to-face with him.

"Hey, it's good to see you again." I tried to keep a cool demeanor though my heart was racing.

"It's good to see you too, Sam." He replied as he looked over my body.

The three girls standing around him looked at me annoyed at my assertiveness.

Luzar stared directly at me with a smirk on his face.

"How you been?" He asked still staring at me.

"I've been good."

"Well, you definitely look good." He leaned towards me.

Johnny was texting on his phone. Likely to Lexi.

Zach and Sophie made their way down the bar to us. He gave me the meanest look realizing that Sophie and I used him, so I could get close to Luzar. I didn't care because it worked and Luzar was showing me more attention than the other girls.

After an hour past, we all decided to hang out in Zach's hotel room.

We sat around on the L-shaped couch in the living room of the suite. This time I was not letting Luzar focus on anyone but me.

I sat really close to him and he put his arm around my waist as Zach told jokes. The three girls Luzar came to the bar with just sat on the other end of the couch glancing

Luzar.

The next night, Sophie and I sat at the band's hotel bar in the first floor lobby waiting for Zach to show up.

"I hope Luzar comes down with him" I said to Sophie.

"He will. Just remember to be brave and go after him."

Sophie looked good tonight. She straightened her hair and donned a dark pink lipstick and black eyeliner with a winged tip. She was obviously wearing a corset under her fitted low-cut top and tight jeans. She looked good with her corseted hour-glass figure, but one could see she was uncomfortable as she sat stiff on the barstool.

She was my wingman tonight. We made a plan that she would distract Zach while I talked to Luzar.

This was my last shot.

My heart pounded in my chest so hard, I could barely catch my breath. My adrenaline was pumping. I had to close my eyes and center myself.

When I felt myself calm down, I opened my eyes and saw Zach making a beeline towards me. I looked to see if Luzar was with him. But, he was alone. I began to worry that seeing Luzar again was not going to happen tonight.

"What's up?" Zach sang out to me as he wrapped his arms around my waist and pressed his pelvis against mine so that I could feel his limp manhood through his pants.

"Hey, Zach. This is my friend, Sophie." I tried to distract him and escape his grasp.

Zach turned to Sophie and introduced himself. I pulled away from him and moved my chair closer to Sophie.

Just as I was about to give up on seeing Luzar tonight, he and Johnny walked up to the bar surrounded by three beautiful women.

I tapped Sophie on the back signaling her to distract

pulled me close to him. He pressed himself firm against my bottom as he wrapped his arms tightly around me.

His manhood grew firmer as he grinded on me. His hot breath was heavy on the back of my neck. I felt scared for what I knew he was expecting from me. I wanted to pull away, but I did not want to offend him. So, I just let him continue.

When the elevator doors opened, Luzar grabbed my hand and guided me to the door of his hotel room.

He was very quiet.

We entered his suite and he did not face me until we were in the bedroom.

I was nervous. So nervous that I just stood there, too stiff to move.

He pulled me closer to him and kissed me. His lips were cold and wet. And, his tongue tasted stale from the drinks he had earlier.

He unzipped my jeans and slid his hand underneath my panties lightly stroking me with his fingers.

He shoved his tongue deeper into my mouth forcing me to open my mouth wider. Some of the saliva from his wet mouth drooled into mine which made me uneasy. Luzar did not seem to notice my uneasiness as he continued his wet kiss.

Then, he lifted my shirt over my head and undid my bra.

With my breast revealed he pinched and pulled at my nipples. I closed my eyes as his cold hands warmed from my body's heat.

As he slid his hand back into my panties to continue stimulating me, I became excited.

I opened my eyes and he was staring back at me. His eyes wide and unblinking with excitement.

He bent down to one knee and took off my shoes then

enviously at me. One of the girls accepted defeat and began flirting with Zach instead.

A knock on the door startled everyone. Johnny opened the door and it was Lexi. He gave her a long hug and they sat in the center of the couch next to Sophie, who sat alone on the couch the whole time we were there. She leaned over and introduced herself to Lexi.

Lexi waved at me when she saw me on the couch. I waved back and quickly turned my attention back to Luzar.

He began kissing my neck and I giggled at the tingling sensation.

"Come up to my room." Luzar whispered. The hairs on the back on my neck stood on end with his warm breath tickling my ear.

"Okay." This was the moment I wanted. To be alone with him.

But, I did not want to be just another groupie he slept with.

I wanted him to take me seriously and see me as girlfriend material.

With the drinks I had earlier, I could not think clearly to make a plan. I knew that if I did not go with him to his room, he would just leave with one of the other girls.

He grabbed my hand and pulled me to my feet. I lost my balance and felt dizzy as I stood up too quickly. He led me to the door.

I looked over at Lexi and Sophie. Lexi had a concerned expression as she gave me a short wave goodbye. Sophie just stared back at me motionless on the couch.

A feeling of dread came over me. But, it was too late to turn back.

Luzar held my hand all the way to the elevator. When we entered the small space, he stood behind me and enviously at me. One of the girls accepted defeat and began flirting with Zach instead.

A knock on the door startled everyone. Johnny opened the door and it was Lexi. He gave her a long hug and they sat in the center of the couch next to Sophie, who sat alone on the couch the whole time we were there. She leaned over and introduced herself to Lexi.

Lexi waved at me when she saw me on the couch. I waved back and quickly turned my attention back to Luzar.

He began kissing my neck and I giggled at the tingling sensation.

"Come up to my room." Luzar whispered. The hairs on the back on my neck stood on end with his warm breath tickling my ear.

"Okay." This was the moment I wanted. To be alone with him.

But, I did not want to be just another groupie he slept with.

I wanted him to take me seriously and see me as girlfriend material.

With the drinks I had earlier, I could not think clearly to make a plan. I knew that if I did not go with him to his room, he would just leave with one of the other girls.

He grabbed my hand and pulled me to my feet. I lost my balance and felt dizzy as I stood up too quickly. He led me to the door.

I looked over at Lexi and Sophie. Lexi had a concerned expression as she gave me a short wave goodbye. Sophie just stared back at me motionless on the couch.

A feeling of dread came over me. But, it was too late to turn back.

Luzar held my hand all the way to the elevator. When we entered the small space, he stood behind me and pulled me close to him. He pressed himself firm against my bottom as he wrapped his arms tightly around me.

His manhood grew firmer as he grinded on me. His hot breath was heavy on the back of my neck. I felt scared for what I knew he was expecting from me. I wanted to pull away, but I did not want to offend him. So, I just let him continue.

When the elevator doors opened, Luzar grabbed my hand and guided me to the door of his hotel room.

He was very quiet.

We entered his suite and he did not face me until we were in the bedroom.

I was nervous. So nervous that I just stood there, too stiff to move.

He pulled me closer to him and kissed me. His lips were cold and wet. And, his tongue tasted stale from the drinks he had earlier.

He unzipped my jeans and slid his hand underneath my panties lightly stroking me with his fingers.

He shoved his tongue deeper into my mouth forcing me to open my mouth wider. Some of the saliva from his wet mouth drooled into mine which made me uneasy. Luzar did not seem to notice my uneasiness as he continued his wet kiss.

Then, he lifted my shirt over my head and undid my bra.

With my breast revealed he pinched and pulled at my nipples. I closed my eyes as his cold hands warmed from my body's heat.

As he slid his hand back into my panties to continue stimulating me, I became excited.

I opened my eyes and he was staring back at me. His eyes wide and unblinking with excitement.

He bent down to one knee and took off my shoes then

he pulled down my jeans. I rested my hands on his shoulders for balance as he pulled each leg of my jeans to the floor.

Still kneeling he slowly slid his hands up my thighs to remove my thong.

I was completely naked.

Luzar was still wearing all of his clothes. I felt awkward standing in front of him. And, he seemed to enjoy this.

He pushed me onto my back on the bed with my legs hanging over the edge so that my feet were flat on the floor. He kneeled to the floor and slid his left arm underneath my hips.

Then, he placed his face between my thighs.

The taste buds of his tongue tickled. The stimulation made my body tingle with pleasure. I felt the warm blood flush my skin.

A groan of pleasure escaped my lips. My body tensed as warm blood flooded my brain making my head feel light as I climaxed.

I laid on the bed trying to catch my breath. Luzar stood over me proud of his accomplishment then began removing his clothes. I continued to lay preparing to let him have his way with my body.

Once he was completely naked, he climbed on top of me and laid all his weight on me. He was lean, but his weight was more than I could bear. I did not move, I let his weight press me into the mattress.

When he kissed me and I tasted myself.

His slim, firm manhood pressed against my inner thigh as he lifted my bottom. The head of his manhood pushed slowly into me. With a steady thrust, he completely entered me.

He exhaled in pleasure. I knew at this moment there

was no going back, and I let him have me.

Each thrust was slow and deep. When he was fully inside me, he would press himself deeper. Every time he pushed deeper into me, his body tensed with a slight shiver.

My mind was active. I laid the palms of my hands on his back and kissed his neck as he continued to thrust. I wanted to make this moment as intimate as I could.

He became firmer and his thrust quickened. I knew he was close to climaxing, so I held him tighter. He reached under me and squeezed my bottom.

I could hear his pelvis clap against my bottom as he thrusted harder. He let out a scream of pleasure as I felt him explode inside of me. He held me tightly for an extra second then he relaxed.

I could still feel him throbbing as he relaxed all his weight onto me.

He lifted his head and stared into my eyes. Smiling at me, he pulled himself from inside me, then rolled onto his back and turned his head to look at me.

"Are you okay?" He asked staring at me.

"Yeah!" My voice cracked.

"Did you enjoy it? You're really quiet." He continued to stare at me which made me stiffen with discomfort.

"I enjoyed it." I quickly replied.

Luzar was right. I felt ashamed that I had been with him so soon. I laid there disappointed with myself.

This did not go the way I imagined.

I wanted to tease him and make him pursue me before giving in to his advances. Everyone knew that the easier you are with these guys, the less they will respect you.

Luzar quietly laid there as he continued to stare at me. I was too afraid to look back at him.

"Um, you want some water?" He asked as he stood from

the bed and walked to the minibar in the living room.

He pulled out two water bottles. I sat up at the edge of the bed. I began putting on my clothes to leave. I felt so awkward, I knew he would likely ask me to leave.

"What are you doing? You're staying the night, RIGHT?" He looked at me confused as he took a sip from his water bottle.

He pulled the covers back on the bed and slid in laying his head on the pillows.

"Come here and lay with me. I like to cuddle." He said smiling and reaching his arms out towards me.

I felt relieved as I put my clothes back on the floor and climbed into the bed.

Luzar pulled the sheets over my body as I rested my head on his chest.

I thought maybe I didn't ruin my chances after all.

10

I felt a tingling sensation as my arm woke up from being trapped under Luzar's body.

He was sleeping so peacefully, I quietly climbed over him to make my way to use the bathroom.

Afterwards, I walked out of the small toilet closet to see Luzar sitting up in the bed texting on his phone. When he saw me approaching the bed, he quickly laid the cell phone on the night stand.

"Morning." He said with a wide grin.

He looked boyish with his dark hair messy and his face flushed.

"Good morning." I tried to sound sultry, but it came out strained from just waking.

"Let's order some breakfast." He picked up a room service menu, "Pancakes and bacon sound good to you?"

"Yes!" I felt I was living in a fantasy because this could not be real.

I relaxed and snuggled under him while he placed our order over phone.

After hanging up the phone he turned to me and gave

me a quick peck on my lips.

"So, what should we do while we wait for breakfast"

He pulled the covers over our heads and climbed on top of me.

"Sorry I left you guys there." I said to Sophie over the phone.

Luzar had to go into the studio with the band to mix the new album.

I was back at my apartment reliving each detail with Sophie.

I had been in a dreamlike state all morning.

Lexi was not back yet, so I assumed she was still with Johnny.

"I'm glad everything worked out like we planned." Sophie was so excited for me. I was glad to have her as my friend.

As I recounted my night with Luzar to her over the phone, I could tell Sophie was sad that her night didn't go so well. She had to leave the hotel alone and intoxicated.

"I still can't believe you hooked up with Luzar!" Sophie squealed.

"Sam, your dreams are coming true. Everything Spring predicted is happening." Sha reminded me.

She was right it was all happening the way Spring predicted.

I heard Lexi walking into the apartment. I told Sophie I would call her back and went into the living room to catch Lexi.

"Hey, how was your night?" I asked Lexi.

"It was good. Did you have fun?" She asked me with a worried expression.

"I really hit it off with Luzar. I feel a strong connection with him." I confided.

Lexi just looked to the side, trying to avoid my eyes as if she was hiding something. "What's up? Did everything go okay with you and Johnny last night?" I asked trying to figure out why Lexi was behaving so odd.

"Everything's good." She stared directly into my eyes, "Be careful with Luzar, Sam. Don't fall for him too quickly."

"What do you mean?" My heart began to race.

"Luzar has a fiancée." She revealed.

"What!? Did Johnny tell you this? Is it his child's mother?" I was confused. I'd cyber stalked Luzar and everyone close to him. But, I never came across a fiancée.

"It's not his child's mother. It's some model in Los Angeles." Lexi said, "They also live together."

Lexi burst my dreamlike state and brought me crashing back to reality.

I wanted to throw something at her. How could she ruin my moment like this?

"Just have fun with him." She added, "Did you have sex with him last night?"

"Yes! And, he didn't use a condom." I was mortified.

"Geez, Sam! He is likely having unprotected sex with a lot of other girls as well."

"I'm on the pill, but I've only been with DJ till this point so a condom didn't register." Tears welled in my eyes.

"The whole night was so perfect, Lexi. He seemed to really like me." The tears spilled over and ran down my cheeks.

"He could care for you, Sam. I'm not saying that he doesn't. You just need to take things slow and protect yourself." Lexi handed me a tissue.

I wiped the tears from my eyes and tried to calm myself.

Lexi and I sat on the couch. She sat patiently as I regained my composure.

"Well, how was your night with Johnny?" I asked trying to change the subject.

"It was good. I really like him! I may be falling for him!" She exclaimed with her eyes wide with excitement.

"Really, do you think he feels the same?" I tried to disguise the envy in my voice, but I was sure she was noticed.

"He said that he was falling in love with me. But, I froze in shock and he got upset that I didn't say it back right away. I don't know what to do." Lexi was beginning to worry.

"Well, be careful. He could be telling every girl he hooks up with that he loves them just to string them along." I wanted to break Lexi's spirit the way she broke mine.

The sharp pain that flashed in her eyes was enough to make me feel better.

"You're right, Sam. These guys can have any girl they want. I'm sure they have girls in every state and possibly every country!" Lexi's upbeat mood was fading.

I decided at that moment I was going to continue pursuing Luzar. If he was serious about his so-called fiancée, he would not have been with me. And, I was definitely not going to allow Lexi to get in my way of what I wanted.

11

I was back at another psychic fare at the trailer in the parking lot. I needed to get more insight from Spring. And, I decided to bring Lexi with me to see what Spring would predict for her.

When I put my name on the list, I noticed Sophie's name towards the top.

After about 30 minutes of waiting, I was called to see Spring.

As I made my way back I saw Sophie with one of the other psychics. She didn't see me, so I just kept walking to Spring's table.

"Hello, again!" Spring said pleasantly.

"Hey." I nervously sat in the metal folding chair praying Spring would tell me how to proceed with Luzar.

"I'm going to use the tarot for you this time."

Spring began shuffling her tarot cards and laid them out onto the tablecloth between her crystals.

She studied the cards for a second then took a deep breath and tilted her head to the side to listen to the invisible being that stood behind her. Then, she brought her attention back to me.

"I see you are in a new space now. You are putting yourself in a position to receive." She paused after this statement. Then, she began again.

"The spirits are telling me that you are close to obtaining a wish, but there are many obstacles. It's surrounding a man. Does this sound familiar?" She looked into my eyes to ensure she was on the right path.

"Yes. I moved out of my home and now have an apartment with a roommate. The guy that I want to be with is here, but I don't know how to make him fall for me." I did not want to give away too many details, but I really needed her guidance.

"The spirits are telling me that you've been intimate with him. I hope I am not overstepping." She said.

"It's okay. I have been intimate with him. I feel a connection, but I'm not sure how he feels."

Spring pulled a few more cards from her deck and laid them on the table.

"He really likes you. But, I do see another woman in his life. Someone he likes as well. She is close to where he lives." Spring laid out more cards, "They have an understanding. She tolerates him being with other girls. This is one of the main reasons he likes her. But, I don't see it lasting long. He gets bored easily."

This was a relief for me. Now, I just needed to know my role in this.

"So, what does this mean for me?"

"He's going to see other women and keep this girl around for a while. You can be sexual with him just make sure to be just his friend. Don't put pressure on him or he will run. It's really up to you where this goes." Spring added another set of cards on the table.

"Also, keep your options open. There are others with

more status who will pursue you."

She paused for a second and tilted her head to listen to the spirit. Then, she studied the cards again. I was on the edge of my seat. I was curious what was being whispered to her.

"There is another man who is close by. He seems somehow connected to the other guy. I see him being a prospect as someone you will become close to. Although you want the other, I see this guy as someone you can build a close bond with. Don't judge him too harshly and try to build a friendship with him as well. I see him benefiting you in some way in the future."

Spring checked her watch and my time was up.

I walked back to the waiting room and felt more confused.

Lexi went back to Spring for her reading and I waited for her outside the trailer.

I was desperate to know what Spring was predicting for her.

Lexi finally came out of the trailer. She had a confused expression as well, and didn't say anything as we walked through the parking lot.

As soon as we climbed into my car, I grilled Lexi for every detail of her reading.

"What did Spring tell you?" I demanded.

"Well, she said that Johnny did have feelings for me and considered me girlfriend material, but he was seeing someone else. She said this girl would be revealed to me." Lexi shook her head.

"Did she say how?" I needed more information.

"No, she told me that I could eventually be his girlfriend, but to just enjoy the intimacy for now and just be his friend." Lexi sighed.

"Are you going to see him tonight?" I asked trying to see

if she would take Spring's advice.

"I guess. I don't know how to feel. I like him and maybe Spring is right." Lexi looked defeated.

I could not help but feel relieved that this relationship could go bad for her.

She could not handle this lifestyle.

"Well, I'm sure it will work out." I said reassuringly.

As soon as the words left my mouth Lexi's phone rang.

"It's Johnny!" She said answering the phone.

Back at the apartment, Lexi went out to meet with Johnny.

I had not heard from Luzar and I wanted to call him. But, I was afraid of coming on too strong, so I tried to wait for him to call me.

After an hour went by, I decided to call Sophie to get her opinion on if I should call him.

"Sam, if you want him, go and get him." She advised, "This is a once in a lifetime opportunity. You can't let it pass."

"You're right. It's just that Johnny called Lexi to come over, why can't Luzar call me?" It bothered me that Lexi did not have to wonder if Johnny liked her, he made it very clear. I wanted the same from Luzar. I wanted him to come after me. Not the other way around.

"Sam, you have to remember that Johnny is not the star of the band. He must make an effort to get girls. Luzar is not used to having to try." Sophie was right, but it did not make me feel any better.

"But, that should not matter. If a man wants you, he will make an effort to see you." I could not shake the feeling that Luzar may not have been as into me as I was into him.

"I understand wanting him to behave more

romantically. But, you don't want to do nothing and always wonder what could have been." Sophie advised, "I think you should text him."

This was exactly what I wanted. Sophie to confirm what I was planning to do anyway. I did not know why I needed her to permit me to text him, but it made me feel less afraid.

"What's the worst that can happen."

Two hours went by since I texted Luzar. He had not texted me back. I was checking my phone constantly, praying he would respond. I even went on his online social profile with my secret page.

I looked through all the band members' pages to see if Luzar was out with them. I could not find anything.

Another hour of waiting, and I had a terrifying feeling that Luzar was not going to respond. My chest felt as if it were caving in. I wanted to cry, but I could barely breathe from the pressure in my lungs.

I tried to focus and figure out what to do next. The obsession of wanting to see him made my mind race. I needed to do something. I could not sit there all night and not be with him. I went over the text I sent him to see if he could have misinterpreted it. I texted him that I wanted to see him again tonight. There was no way to misinterpret that message.

I decided to text Lexi. Maybe they were all hanging out and she could invite me over.

Sam: Hey, Lexi. What's going on? Are you guys hanging out with Luzar? Call me.

Another hour went by, and now Lexi was not texting me back.

I was fully dressed in my favorite dark blue skinny jeans and red crop top. I even curled my hair and did my make-up in case Luzar or Lexi called to invite me over.

I was so angry at Lexi for not texting me back. I could not understand what was so special about her. Why did I have to go through her to get invited to hang with the band? I was more attractive and had a better personality.

I decided to text Lexi again.

Sam: Lexi, what's up? Are you guys hanging out at the hotel rooftop bar? Is it okay if I come up? Call me.

It was after 10 o'clock at night, and I still did not hear anything from Lexi or Luzar. I was going crazy. My head was pounding from the anxiety. I had to do something.

So, I called Sophie again. She was the only person I could get in touch with.

"No one's texting me back!" I cried to Sophie over the phone. The stress was too much to bear and I became emotional.

"What's going on?" Sophie was concerned.

"I texted Lexi twice and she didn't text me back!" My voice was strained as I tried to talk through my tears.

"Sam, Lexi only cares about herself. She should have at least texted you back."

"That should be me hanging with them, not her!" I was crying louder.

"What if she is ignoring me on purpose? Remember what Spring said to me about her being out for herself?" I reminded Sophie.

"I remember, Sam. You need to get Lexi out of your way."

"Do you think I should text Luzar again?" I asked Sophie, though I knew it was a bad idea.

"No. You will appear needy if you do." I was afraid she would say this.

"I know. You're right. Let me call you back, I'm going to try texting Lexi again." I needed to get Sophie off the phone. She was not helping me get to Luzar. The only person who could help me was Lexi.

I decided not to text Lexi, but to call her instead. It rang a few times, then went to her voicemail.

"Hey, girl! What's going on? Are you guys hanging out? Is Luzar there? Call me back! I really need to talk to you!"

Two more hours went by, and it was after midnight.

My head pounded as I tried to lay down, but the tension would not allow me to relax.

I decided to go onto my fake online social profile again.

I checked the band members' pages and even checked their friends' pages. I could not find any trace of Luzar.

I buried my face into my pillow, wondering why this was happening to me.

I opened my eyes to the sun peering through my window blinds.

"Oh no!" I fell asleep.

My heart raced as I checked my phone to see if I missed any text messages from Luzar or Lexi. But, there were no messages on my phone.

I felt empty inside. I cried so much last night, that I could not feel any emotions. I was too exhausted.

I still had on my clothes that I planned to wear to see Luzar last night. My makeup was smeared on my light blue pillowcase.

Once this state past, my first instinct was to text Lexi.

Sam: What happened last night? Did you guys hang out? Was Luzar there?

* * *

I slid to the edge of my bed and let my legs hang over. I saw all my dreams of being Luzar's girlfriend painfully moving out of reach. I could not understand why Luzar did not text me back.

My phone chimed, indicating that I received a message. My heart raced as I clambered to open my phone's screen to view the message. I prayed it was Luzar. But, my excitement quickly turned into a worse sadness when I saw the message was from Sophie.

Sophie: Did you hear from Luzar?

I did not text her back. I decided to send Lexi another text instead.

Sam: Hey Lexi. Was Luzar out with you and Johnny last night? Is everything okay? Text me back.

I looked at my phone's clock and it was 9 o' clock in the morning. I decided to check the band's social media page. There was no evidence of them being out last night.

I paced in my room trying to decide what I needed to do to find out why no one was calling me back.

I called Lexi's phone again.

I realized I was desperate, but I needed to know what was going on.

"Lexi it's Sam. Call me back. I'm losing my mind over here." I tried to sound normal on Lexi's voicemail, but I was a wreck.

I caught a glimpse of myself in the mirror. I looked horrible. My lipstick was smeared across my cheek and my mascara had run into the creases of my under eye bags which were swollen from crying. I needed to get myself together.

As I started towards my bathroom, my phone rang.

It was Lexi.

12

"I left my purse in the living room of Johnny's suite." Lexi explained, "He told me my phone was chiming all night."

"What?! Does he know it was me?" I was mortified.

"Yeah. He asked me who was calling and texting all night." Lexi said.

"And you told him it was me?" I was furious with her.

"Sam, I have a ton of texts and missed calls from you. Who was I supposed to say they were from."

I was so embarrassed.

I knew he would tell Luzar about this. Lexi had just ruined everything for me.

I wondered if she did this on purpose.

"So, what happened last night? Luzar never called me. Did you see him?" I was pissed at her, but I was still curious about what Luzar was doing.

"No, we didn't see Luzar. Johnny and I stayed in all night. We just ordered room service."

"Do you know if Luzar was with another girl last night?"

"I didn't see any of the other band members. I was only

with Johnny all night." I could hear the annoyance in her voice.

"Okay. Well, let me call you back." I hung up the phone before she could respond.

I could not believe she showed Johnny my messages. She was supposed to help me get with Luzar. That was the only reason I moved in with her.

I decided to take a shower and pull myself together. I redid my makeup, brushed out my hair, and put on a yellow sundress with tiny red roses on it. I thought wearing something bright might lighten my mood.

I made some coffee, sat on the couch, and turned on the television while I waited for Lexi to come back to the apartment. This was not over. I was going to find a way to bring Luzar back to me.

Lexi walked into the apartment carrying her overnight bag.

It was just after 4 o'clock in the afternoon. Her hair was in a ponytail and her face was bare.

She startled when she saw me sitting on the couch. Her expression was that of someone who was caught in a wrongful act.

"Hey!" She said as her flip flops dragged the floor while she walked to her bedroom.

She wore black yoga pants and a basic white t-shirt. She always dressed plain, never putting any effort into her look.

I followed Lexi into her room. She removed the clothes from her overnight bag and put them into a dirty clothes hamper.

"So, how was your night?" I leaned in the doorway with my arms crossed over my chest.

"It was good. Johnny and I just chilled in his hotel room

and watched movies." She said as she continued removing items from her large bag.

"So, you didn't hang with any of the other band members last night?" I had a feeling Lexi was hiding something from me.

"No, it was just Johnny and myself all night." Lexi said distracted by the contents in her bag.

I caught a glimpse of a large black box with a white ribbon. Lexi tried to hide the box from my view.

"So, what else did you guys do today?" I said motioning at the package in her bag.

"We went out this morning and just hung out." Lexi was trying to avoid my eyes.

"So, he took you shopping this morning. There's only one place that packages items in black boxes wrapped with a white ribbon." I wondered why Lexi was hiding the box from me.

I marched to the bag and pulled the package from Lexi's bag. It was a huge box, so it was likely a purse.

"Is this a purse? Open it! Let me see!" I demanded.

Lexi quickly snatched the package from me and put it in her closet and closed the sliding door.

"I'm not ready to open it just yet. I want to do an unboxing video." She said slamming her closet door shut.

"Jeez, okay!" I said throwing my hands up in surrender.

"Look, I just walked in Sam. Let me relax and we can talk later. Okay?"

I decided not to argue with her and left her room. She closed the bedroom door behind me. I thought she was being dramatic. But, I also could not wrap my head around her getting an expensive purse.

With my ego bruised, I went into my room and called Sophie to vent.

"I don't get it." I complained to Sophie over the phone,

"She's not that attractive."

"Sam, she's just having sex with this guy. And, you must remember he's the bass player. You were with the lead singer." Sophie tried to make me feel better.

"But, I had sex with Luzar and he's ignoring me." I felt worse as I remembered sitting by the phone alone last night.

"Sam, the only thing you need to focus on is using Lexi to get to Luzar." Sophie said.

"How, Sophie? She's not even hanging with the other band members."

"Get her to invite you over there tomorrow night. And, find a way to make yourself the center of attention. You are way more beautiful and stylish. Just box her out."

Sophie sighed.

"Look Sam. I'm here for you, but I have a lot going on right now. I really need to get off the phone."

The next day, Lexi and I were scheduled to work at the department store. It was a slow morning and I had not seen her all day.

During my lunch break, I decided to go to the men's department to find her. She was in a corner of the department folding shirts.

"Hey, take your break now." I demanded.

"I have to finish folding these shirts." She rolled her eyes at me.

I was determined to get her alone. So, I quickly helped her fold the remainder of the shirts. I grabbed her arm and pulled her to walk with me. We went into the mall area.

We ordered drinks and sat at a table in a coffee shop.

I sized her up. She had a blemish-free medium brown complexion. Her body was not as fit as mine, but she had bigger breasts. She was confident, but not enough to put any effort into her style.

"Why don't you tell Johnny you want to go out on a double date with Luzar and me?" I waited to see how she would react.

"What?!" Lexi squinted her eyes in confusion.

"Lexi, I want to get to know Luzar better. He isn't contacting me, and I really like him." I pleaded with Lexi.

"Okay, Sam. I'll talk to Johnny and see if he will agree to it. But, I think you're wasting your time on Luzar." Lexi said, "I'll call Johnny after work."

"No! Text him, now!" My forcefulness made her jump slightly in the chair.

I grabbed Lexi's purse and pulled out her phone. She looked at me bewildered. I did not care. I needed this to happen.

She shook her head in disbelief, and started texting Johnny.

"Make sure he agrees to bring Luzar." I said.

Forcing Lexi to text Johnny worked. She texted me later that day that Luzar and Johnny wanted to go out to dinner with us tonight.

Finally.

I needed to look my best tonight. I spent the remainder of the day at work imagining what I should wear.

I decided on my dark blue spaghetti strap dress with the low-cut V-neck line and my padded bra that made my breasts look two sizes bigger.

I could not wait to get home to start getting ready.

When I came home from work, I decided to look up Luzar's fiancée on the internet.

There were a lot of pictures of her. I still could not believe I knew nothing about her.

She was a typical California blond surfer girl who

rarely wore makeup.

She was the complete opposite of Luzar. He was dark and emo, with dark eyeliner, and black clothes. I never would have guessed she was his type.

After looking through a lot of her pictures, I toned down my makeup and just wore concealer, mascara, and tented lip gloss.

I checked myself in the mirror. I felt odd without my complicated eyeshadow and colorful lipstick. But, if this was what Luzar was attracted to, then it was worth a shot.

"Lexi are you almost ready?" I yelled as I walked through our living room to Lexi's bedroom.

She was still straightening her hair. I went back into the living room and sat on the sofa to wait for her to finish.

Lexi finally came out of her room. She wore a white fitted top with a low scoop-neck line. This was tucked into a pair of dark blue skinny jeans paired with black flat sandals. Lexi even wore a bronzy foundation with a plum colored lipstick.

She looked good, it seemed the guys in this band preferred plain and natural.

Lexi pulled up to the hotel and Johnny jumped into the back seat, then leaned forward to kiss her.

"Hey, Sam." He said just to acknowledge me being in the car.

Lexi drove off toward Midtown.

"Luzar and Craig are following us in the SUV." Johnny called out.

"What?!" I exclaimed looking back. Johnny looked back at me with a snarl, but he didn't respond.

Lexi looked over at me with her eyes wide with

confusion. Craig coming along was a surprise to her as well. I wondered if this was a joke. Why would Craig come on our double date?

Lexi turned into the restaurant's parking lot and I saw Luzar and Craig getting out of a black SUV.

My knees started shaking when I stepped onto the pavement. I was nervous and felt as if something bad was going to happen tonight.

I looked back at Lexi, looped my arm through hers, and held her close to me as we walked into the restaurant.

Johnny walked ahead of us to catch up with Luzar and Craig.

When Johnny was out of hearing range I turned to Lexi.

"Did you know Craig was coming?" I asked her.

"I had no idea. I don't understand why Craig is here."

"I'm afraid to go in there. Maybe this is a bad idea and I should go home." I stopped and turned to walk back into the parking lot.

Lexi stopped me.

"You like Luzar and you did nothing with Craig. You did nothing to be ashamed of. Just ignore Craig. Okay." Lexi said holding my shoulders and trying to console me.

"You're right, I did nothing wrong." I took a deep breath and walked with Lexi arm in arm into the restaurant.

The restaurant was styled like a café with a full menu. There was a large oval bar with a dessert and coffee serving section on one side and alcoholic beverages on the other. Small café style tables and chairs were in the coffee/dessert section, and a separate room behind the bar had larger dinner tables.

As we all stood at the hostess stand waiting to be seated, Luzar glanced at me and stood awkwardly beside Craig.

"Hey, Sam!" He called out with a mischievous smirk.

"Hey." I responded meekly.

I stayed close to Lexi as the hostess guided us to a table in the back corner of the restaurant. Johnny pulled Lexi to the chair next to him which left me sitting next to Luzar across from Lexi. Craig sat at the end of the square table by Luzar and Johnny.

Sitting next to Luzar, my body was tensed. I wanted to talk to him, but I could not get a clear thought.

Meanwhile, Johnny and Lexi were all over each other.

He had his arm around her waist and held her so tightly she had to lean onto her hip. They even read off the same menu.

Everyone ignored me at the table. I just sat there feeling like an outcast.

While the guys continued to talk, Lexi turned to face me and nudged her head towards Luzar encouraging me to talk to him. I scrunched my shoulders upward indicating to her that I was trying but did not know what to say. Johnny mentioned an artist whose paintings he liked.

"Oh, you know Sam paints." Lexi chimed in.

Everyone at the table stared at her in silence. She looked at me urging me to say something.

"Oh, you're a painter? That's interesting." Luzar finally turned toward me.

"Yes. I am trying to build a collection of work." I said nervously.

"That's really cool! You have to show me your work." Luzar seemed intrigued.

"Definitely." I regained the confidence back in my voice.

I mentally thanked Lexi.

My nerves began to calm and Luzar looked at me. I smiled at him, then he smiled back.

We were having a moment until Craig obnoxiously cleared his throat.

I almost forgot he was sitting at the end of the table.

Our waitress, a petit blond, was grinning from ear to ear at the excitement of the band members sitting in her section. Her body awkwardly rocked from side to side as she stood at the table.

"Hey guys! My name is Lola. Can I get y'all started with some drinks?" She said in a thick southern accent.

The guys did not seem fazed by the waitress' odd behavior. I'm sure they experienced this a lot.

After we ordered our drinks, the guys started talking amongst themselves again. So, I used this opportunity to signal Lexi to come with me to the ladies' restroom.

We excused ourselves from the table and walked into the bar area. As Lexi and I walked between the tables past the dessert display, two women with exotic Afro-Asian features and wearing short bodycon dresses stared at us as we past them.

"Them bitches ain't all that." One of them commented in our direction.

Lexi and I ignored them and continued walking through the restroom door.

I stood in front of a row of three sinks and checked my reflection in the mirror.

"Do you think Luzar likes me?" I asked Lexi while she was in the restroom stall.

"He seems interested. I think Craig is cock-blocking though." She said.

"You're SO right! Why is he here?"

"It is weird with him at the table like a fifth wheel." Lexi exited the stall and washed her hands.

"It is a little uncomfortable trying to get Luzar's attention with Craig here."

"Just focus on Luzar and ignore Craig." Lexi advised.

We took another look at our reflections and left the restroom making our way back to our table.

We noticed the two mean girls were not at their table. When we entered the separate dining room, Lexi looked back at me with an annoyed.

I looked ahead of her and the two women were sitting in our chairs flirting with the band members.

They were giggling and leaning over to show the cleavage spilling out, clearly enjoying their invasion of our table.

The guys found this aggressiveness amusing.

Johnny looked at Lexi nervously with a strained smile as we approached the table.

The two girls kept their backs turned to us and continued to talk to the guys.

Lexi walked around the table to Johnny's side and looked sternly at the girls.

"Take your rude, raggedy asses back to your table!" Lexi yelled loudly at the girls.

"Who do you think you talking to?" The girl next to Johnny called out.

"I'm obviously talking to YOU, dumb ass!" Lexi's body tensed as she balled up her fists, as if preparing for a physical altercation.

Our waitress rushed over to the table. Johnny jumped up and held Lexi's arms to prevent her from swinging her fists at the intruders.

"Hey babe. We're just having a laugh. It's not serious!" Johnny said blocking her from the two girls who were now standing and approaching Lexi.

I moved next to our waitress who stood at the other end of the table. She was wide-eyed in disbelief of what she was witnessing.

Luzar and Craig just sat in their chairs stunned at Lexi's outburst. Customers sitting at nearby tables stared curiously at the commotion.

Lexi did not care.

Her skin blushed red as she became enraged.

She and the two girls yelled insults at each other. They were so loud and their words overlapped that I could not make out what they were saying.

"What's the problem here?" A deep authoritative, male voice called out behind me.

A man about mid-thirties wearing a button-up white shirt rushed to the table. He was the restaurant's manager.

"There's no problem, sir. These ladies are leaving." Luzar said calmly pointing at the two girls being pushed back by Johnny trying to protect Lexi.

"Hey ladies!" Luzar called out to the two women. "It was nice meeting you, we're going to finish our drinks now. Have a nice evening."

I was still standing next to the waitress when the girls walked by. One shoved my chair making it hit my legs. She walked slowly past me staring into my eyes, daring me to say something to her. I stepped back allowing her and her friend to pass.

Craig started laughing hysterically at the ordeal.

"This is too much!" Craig said between his laughter, shaking his head.

"Why did you let that bitch sit in my chair?" Now, Lexi was turning her anger onto Johnny.

"They were fans. It was harmless Lexi." Johnny held his hands up in surrender.

Lexi walked back around the table to her chair and I meekly sat back in mine next to Luzar.

Lexi sat with her arms crossed and her lips pouting

while Johnny continued consoling her.

"Hey, let's head back to the hotel." Luzar whispered in my ear.

Still shaken, I just nodded my head yes.

"Drinks are on me guys." Luzar signaled to the waitress to bring the bill.

As we walked out of the restaurant, I fell more in love with Luzar. Especially after watching him take control of the situation with the two girls.

He was definitely a leader.

13

I decided to ride with Luzar and Craig since Johnny and Lexi started arguing again in the parking lot at the restaurant.

It felt good to sit in the passenger seat next to Luzar. Craig was a gentleman and sat in the back seat behind me. I did not say much as they talked about random things.

When we stepped out of the SUV, I saw Johnny and Lexi walking into the hotel.

"You guys got here fast!" Luzar called out to them.

We all piled into the elevator.

Johnny and Lexi huddled together in the corner and began kissing.

They made up fast.

When the elevator reached Luzar's floor, Craig followed us into the hallway.

I assumed his suite was on the same floor. But, when we came to Luzar's door, Craig was standing behind us.

Luzar turned to me, "Craig's gonna hang out with us for a little bit."

I felt uncomfortable, but decided to go into Luzar's suite with him and Craig anyway.

"We didn't get a chance to eat anything at the restaurant because of loud mouth Lexi. Let's order some room service. Sam, pick out whatever you want." Luzar handed me the menu.

I sat on the small couch in the living room area and turned on the television. As I looked over the menu, Luzar and Craig pulled out little bottles of liquor from the minibar fridge. Craig started making cocktails with the little bottles.

Luzar walked back to the couch and stood behind me massaging my shoulders.

"You know what you want?" Luzar asked tightening his grip on my shoulders.

"Yeah, the double cheese burger with sweet potato fries." I handed Luzar the menu.

I did not want to look at him.

The way he rubbed my shoulders made my body stiffen with discomfort. I felt a knot grow in my stomach like a warning that something was about to happen.

Luzar ordered double cheese burgers and sweet potato fries for each of us.

"Here's your drink." I was startled and turned around on the couch to see Craig standing behind me with a drink in his hand.

He stared back at me with a blank expression.

I took the drink from his hand and he turned back toward the minibar.

I pretended to be interested in the images on the television.

The energy in the room was tense.

Luzar and Craig spoke to each other in a low voice, so I could not make out their words. I knew I should leave, but my body felt glued to the couch and I was afraid to move.

I finally drummed up the courage to stand from the couch, then room service knocked on the door.

The young man rolled the cart with our food directly in front of me.

I sank back into the couch and prayed I didn't make a bad choice in staying.

After eating our burgers and having a few of Craig's cocktails, we all got along well.

Craig was funny as he told jokes making Luzar and I laugh hysterically. I relaxed and forgot about my suspicions of being in the suite alone with them.

Luzar sat next to me with his arm over my shoulders. Craig was in an arm chair adjacent to us.

"I have to use the toilet, be right back." Luzar sat his glass on the coffee table and walked into the bedroom.

"So, how you been?" Craig asked, taking another sip of his drink.

"I've been good. How have you been?"

"Missing you." Craig stared at me seductively.

His statement shocked me, but I decided to blow it off.

"I really like you, Sam. You're really beautiful." Craig continued.

I did not respond to him. I looked at the bedroom door hoping Luzar would walk back in and interrupt Craig's advances.

Craig stood from his chair and walked toward me. He sat close to me on the couch. So close that our thighs touched. He slid his arm between my back and the couch and pulled me close to him.

"What are you two doing?" Luzar was looming over us from behind the couch. I was too busy trying to avoid Craig, I did not hear Luzar come back into the living room.

"I was telling Sam how beautiful she is." Craig said to Luzar without taking his eyes off me.

"Sam is very beautiful." Luzar said placing his hands on my shoulders.

Luzar, still standing behind me, slid his left hand down the front of my dress and cupped my breast. Then, Craig, still holding me, started kissing my neck.

The caresses felt so good. I became excited as my body tingled from the sensations of them touching me.

Luzar climbed over the back of the couch, sandwiching me between he and Craig.

He placed my hand over the front of his jeans.

"See how much you turn me on, Sam." Luzar said as he turned my face to him and kissed me.

As Luzar and I made out, Craig pulled down the front of my dress and unhooked my bra exposing my breasts.

A part of me wanted this.

The way they kissed and touched me felt so good.

Luzar stood up, grabbed my hand and pulled me to my feet.

He guided me into the dimly lit bedroom with Craig following close behind.

The only light came from the partially closed door of the bathroom.

I began to tremble as we moved closer to the bed.

Luzar gently laid me onto my back. Then, they both laid on either side of me.

They resumed kissing over my body as I continued to tremble from the fear of this new experience.

"Are you okay?" Luzar whispered into my ear as he caressed the side of my face.

"I've never done anything like this."

Craig stopped kissing my neck and looked down at me.

"We're gonna take care of you. We both really like you

Sam." Luzar said in his soft, deep voice.

Craig just laid still on his side staring at me as Luzar and I kissed.

Before my body trembled in fear, now it was trembling with pleasure.

Craig started kissing me as well.

Luzar kneeled to the floor and placed his head between my thighs bringing an overwhelming sensation that made my body spasm uncontrollably.

Then, for a moment, the world did not exist as groans of passion escaped me.

Sensing that I climaxed, Luzar climbed back on the bed and laid next to me.

Before Luzar could kiss me, Craig grabbed my face and kissed me.

His kiss was deep.

Luzar did not protest. He just laid on his side and watched us.

Craig rolled on top of me and his weight pressed me into the mattress.

"I've wanted to do this since I met you." Craig said with a breathy whisper.

Once my body relaxed, his thrusts became smooth and rhythmic. He ran his fingers through my hair and I rested my head in his large hand.

He thrusted deeper into me as he came closer to ecstasy. He kissed me and released a low, throaty moan into my mouth. Then, I felt his warmth inside me.

Craig relaxed his body on top of me putting more pressure and pressing me deeper into the mattress.

He continued to kiss me.

Exhausted, he gasped for air between each kiss as I felt his heart pounding on my chest.

Luzar grabbed my hand, but I was so lost in Craig that I

forgot he was still lying beside us.

With Craig still lying on top of me, I strained to turn my head to look at Luzar.

He stared blankly back at me and at that moment, I felt nothing for Luzar. His eyes were so cold and uncaring.

"Come here!"

Luzar shoved Craig off me and wrapped his arm around my waist, pulling my body to him.

His thrust was hard and fast like a dog in heat.

He even arched his back upward in an unnatural contortion.

Craig stood up and grabbed his arm, stopping him.

He jumped up and brushed past Craig to the toilet, slamming the bathroom door behind him.

"Are you okay?" Craig looked at me concerned.

"I'm fine." I said trying to hold back my tears.

Craig sat beside me and put his arm around my shoulders. We both sat there in silence.

I could see him staring at me from the corner of my eyes.

"Okay, party's over! Thanks for the fun, it's time to go!" Luzar yelled to us as he stormed from the bathroom.

Luzar climbed into the bed and turned on the television with the remote.

Craig helped me fix my dress and found my shoes

Luzar sneered at us, shaking his head.

"Don't be such a jerk, dude!" Craig yelled at Luzar.

"I'm not being a jerk. It was fun. Now, it's time for you both to go. I have a right to tell you to leave." Luzar was so nonchalant in his reaction.

He laid back on a pillow and flipped through the television channels. He pretended to ignore us as we left the bedroom.

"Hey, you can shower in my suite if you want." Craig

offered as he pulled his shirt over his head.
All I could do was nod my head yes.

14

I stood in the shower at Craig's hotel room. I was motionless as I recounted each moment of the night. The warm water felt comforting.

I could not understand what happened to make the night end up this way. Before tonight, Luzar seemed so into me. It was as if he was a different person. His eyes were so dark and menacing. What changed?

I stepped out of the shower and wrapped the large towel around my body. I was thankful Craig was here to comfort me.

I dried myself and put on a terry cloth robe Craig laid out on the bed.

I wondered how I could have been so stupid. Now, I will always be the groupie they had in a threesome. Everything I did was for this opportunity to be with Luzar. And, somehow, it's now ruined.

I walked into the living room and Craig was sitting on the couch watching television.

"Hey, thanks for letting me use your shower."

It was difficult for me to look at him after our

encounter.

"It's fine." He looked at me with concern, "You can stay the night here. It's really late."

"I don't know. I'm just..." I stuttered nervously.

"Hey, it's okay. Stay here tonight." Craig stood up and walked to me. He wrapped his arms around me and kissed my forehead.

The next morning, I woke to Craig spooning me. His breath tickled the back of my neck as he snored softly.

I was so relaxed lying with him I almost forgot about the night before.

I laid still in Craig's arms, as I was not ready to face reality just yet.

I wondered if Craig could be 'The One'. What if we were destined to fall in love?

Being around Luzar would be difficult, but we could make this work. Craig did defend me against Luzar's aggressiveness last night.

As I daydreamed about a future with Craig, I felt him waking up. He stretched out his body and let out a deep yawn, then playfully squeezed me in his arms and kissed the back of my neck.

I rolled onto my back and gazed into his large brown eyes. I could tell he liked me as he looked down at me smiling sweetly.

He swept my hair behind my ear and kissed me softly.

"Let's take a shower and go out for some food." He hopped out of the bed.

He slid his arms under my back and knees, then lifted me from the bed carrying me to the shower.

Craig came with me to my apartment so I could change clothes before we went to breakfast.

He looked at some of the pictures on my dresser.

"Are you close with your family?" He asked sitting on my bed.

"Sort of. My sister gives me a hard time." I confessed as I buttoned my blue jean shirt and tucked it into my white skinny jeans.

"Are you close with your family?"

"I'm close to my mom and little brother, but I rarely see my dad." Craig revealed.

I was not expecting him to be so open about himself.

It was refreshing.

"So, you're a mamma's boy!" I teased him.

"Maybe." He said laughing, "Are you ready yet? I'm starving."

Craig laid back onto my bed. He looked so adorable.

I still secretly wished he was Luzar. I hated myself for thinking this. I really wanted to love Craig, and I'm sure one day I could.

A part of him reminded me of DJ.

He was so talented and had the potential to become great, but he did not have the ambition to be great, like Luzar.

Honestly, if Luzar left the band, Craig would be a nobody. And, I would be a nobody's girlfriend.

I decided we should eat brunch at a hip spot in Little Five Points in East Atlanta.

I knew people in this area would recognize Craig and likely take pictures of us together.

And, I was right.

After parking my car and walking up the crowded, narrow street of boutique stores and restaurants, people gawked at us. Some even stopped us to take pictures with him.

People even took pictures of me and commented on how beautiful and stylish I was.

This felt amazing. I was finally in my element.

The hostess at the small boutique restaurant strategically set us in the middle of the dining area where everyone could see us. It was a way to get the restaurant more popularity.

I did not mind because I enjoyed the attention

I looked over at Craig, and he seemed uncomfortable. He sat across from me with his back hunched over and head down as if he were trying to hide in the middle of the restaurant."Let's sit somewhere more private." He suggested as he started to lift his hand to wave at the hostess.

"I'm fine here. Let them stare, Craig. You're a rock star." I replied as I stopped him from signaling the hostess.

Throughout the brunch, Craig barely spoke to me.

Every time I tried to start a conversation, he would shut it down with quick one-word replies.

I wanted everyone to see Craig being infatuated with me, the way he had been this morning. Instead, he just ignored me and stared into space.

After breakfast, outside the restaurant, Craig stormed off in front of me.

Some of the people passing us on the sidewalk noticed and stared at us curiously.

"Hey, Craig! What's wrong!" I tried to slow him down by grabbing his arm.

"I'm just ready to go!" He snapped at me.

Craig's face turned red and perspiration formed in little dots on this forehead. He snatched his arm from my grasp and stood at the passenger door of my car with his back to me.

I looked around and some of the onlookers laughed, while others looked at me with pity.

I pressed the remote button to unlock the car doors and walked quickly to the driver's side and climbed into the car.

I was shaking so much from embarrassment that I could barely get my key into the ignition.

"Craig, what's wrong?" I asked as he slouched in the passenger seat.

"Nothing, just take me back to the hotel." He said in a low depressing tone.

"But, I don't understand what happened?" I tried to calm him and get him to talk to me.

"I don't want to talk. Just take me to back to the hotel." He demanded, looking straight ahead.

I pulled the car out from the metered parking spot and drove towards his hotel.

Craig was quiet the whole ride in my car. He sat slouched over and staring out of the window.

I didn't try to talk to him because I was afraid he would snap at me again.

As we turned onto the street of his hotel, I did not want him to leave upset. I wanted to resolve whatever happened to make him so upset.

"Do you want me to come up?" I asked him nervously.

"No. Just drop me off at the corner." He said sternly.

"Craig, what happened? Why are you so angry?" I tried to sound calm, but I knew my voice was trembling.

"Pull over here. Just pull over. I'll walk the rest of the way." He pointed at the sidewalk two blocks from his hotel.

I pulled over to the curb and he jumped out while the car was still rolling to a stop.

I sat in the car and watched in disbelief as he stormed

down the street toward his hotel.

"Oh, Sam! I can't believe he did that to you!" Lexi exclaimed after I told her about Craig's behavior earlier that day.

I decided not to tell her about the threesome from fear of her judging me.

"I thought you were with Luzar. How did you end up with Craig?" Lexi asked with a confused expression.

"I didn't hit it off with Luzar. Craig seemed more mature and I felt a stronger connection with him." I lied. I did not want to admit that Luzar kicked me out of his room after I was with both of them.

"Well, Johnny and I got into an argument last night. So, you and I are in the same boat, girl." Lexi revealed.

"I didn't think it would be this hard to date someone famous." She sighed heavily.

"Yeah, neither did I."

15

"Have you heard from him?" I sat at my laptop searching through all of Luzar's and Craig's friend's pages under my fake social profile.

"No. And, I refuse to text him first." Lexi said stubbornly.

Lexi and I had not heard from either Johnny nor Craig since we last saw them.

It was 10:00 pm and we were curious if they were out and if so, were there any pictures posted of them?

I typed in their profile names and hashtags to see if maybe some fans had posted any pictures of them.

"I wonder what they did last night?" Lexi inquired as she sat on the bed behind me and looked over my shoulder at my laptop screen.

"I'll find out. I'm like a detective with this thing. I find everything." I said.

"Okay, detective Sam!" Lexi laughed hysterically.

I combed through each picture looking for details to see if they were recent or not.

Lexi and I sat like this for almost an hour until I found a pic of a girl who looked familiar.

"Is that one of the girls from the restaurant?" Lexi pointed at the picture of a girl that resembled one of the exotic girls we encountered in the cafe style restaurant when we were with Luzar, Johnny, and Craig.

I clicked on her profile name and went through her pictures.

It was definitely the girl from the restaurant. I will never forget her and Lexi almost getting into a fight.

Lexi stood up from the bed.

"That's the girl that was sitting in my chair!" She yelled out with a disgusted expression on her face.

I magnified one of the pictures, and there they were, Johnny and Craig.

I looked through the girl's pictures and they were in most of her pictures.

There were pictures of them at a dance club, at the band's hotel rooftop bar, and even in Craig's suite.

My heart felt as if a weight had crushed it. I was shocked at the pictures I witnessed on the girl's profile page.

Then, there was a picture of the girl in only a white t-shirt sitting on Johnny's bed in his suite with him sleeping next to her.

"He told me he loved me!" Lexi cried out.

Lexi gasped for air between her tears.

I felt bad for her having to witness this.

"Hey, Lexi. He's an asshole. That girl is not on your level. You are way classier and prettier than her." I tried to console Lexi.

Lexi calmed a little and wiped away her tears.

"I'm sorry Sam. I just didn't expect to see that." She said sitting calmly back onto my bed.

"Hey, don't apologize. I understand."

I continued looking through the girl's profile pictures. I

even went through the profiles of her friends to see if I could find more pictures of Craig. But, only Johnny had an intimate picture.

I was relieved.

I felt bad for Lexi, but at least Craig was not as stupid as Johnny. He obviously did not care about her.

"Lexi, I'm sorry for what Johnny did to you, but I am still going to stay friends with them. Craig did not go as far as Johnny did. So, this is between you and him, and I can't be dragged into the middle of it."

I did not want to lose my connections with the band because of Lexi's drama with Johnny.

Lexi sat on my bed and stared blankly at me for a moment.

"Whatever, Sam." She uttered as she stood from my bed.

Her eyes were bloodshot and swollen from crying. She brushed past me and walked back to her room.

I did not feel bad about my decision to stay friends with the band. I wanted Craig and to build something with him. My only purpose for being in that apartment with Lexi was for my advancement, not hers.

I had to remember that.

Lexi didn't speak to me the rest of the night.

I called Sophie and told her everything that happened.

I had to admit I was enjoying Lexi's fall from Johnny's grace.

"Sam, you did the right thing. Her relationship with the bassist of the band is not your problem." Sophie advised, "You can't let her stand in your way of living the life you deserve. It's not your problem she couldn't keep him happy."

"You're right, Sophie. I'm sure she'll get over it."

But, there was one issue. Craig was not returning my

messages.

"Sophie, what should I do about Craig? This is the band's last night here and I haven't heard from him."

I confided to Sophie about hooking up with Craig, but I did not tell her about the threesome with him and Luzar. I was planning to take that experience to the grave.

"Sam, you were with Luzar first and Craig may be struggling with being in Luzar's shadow. He may feel insecure about this."

I believed she was right.

Luzar was the star of the band and Craig was in his shadow. I thought that was the reason he was so upset because I wanted Luzar first.

"Just give him time. Even if he doesn't call, still stay open for contact with him in the future. And, remember what Spring said 'Be his friend'." Sophie reminded me.

After I hung up with Sophie, I decided to have a psychic reading with Spring over the phone. I needed some clarification on what to do.

Her phone readings were expensive with a 15-minute reading costing $60. But, I was losing my mind with everything that happened.

I called Spring and made an appointment for the next day, when I knew the band would be going back to Los Angeles.

After scheduling my psychic reading, I texted Craig again. I wanted to see him so badly before they left the next day.

I heard Lexi's shower come on from her bathroom. It was after 11 o'clock at night. I knew she was getting ready to see Johnny. I could not believe she was seeing him after seeing the pictures of him with the other woman.

I was furious.

I had not heard anything from Craig.

I paced in my room as I waited for her to come out of her bathroom.

When I heard her shower turn off, I rushed into the living room to face her. She quickly stepped out of the bathroom and into her room.

I practically ran to her room to catch her before she could close her door.

"So, you going to see Johnny?" I blurted out.

"We talked. He wants to talk about what happened last night." She said looking at me with surprise and annoyance at my intrusion.

You're really going over there after he disrespected you with that skank groupie?" I said disapprovingly.

"Sam, I do like him. And, it's not like he and I made a commitment to each other. I'm taking this one day at a time." Lexi said holding her towel around her chest.

With her free hand, she pulled a pair of light blue jeans and a red crop-top from her dresser and laid them on the bed.

"Well, don't let him take advantage of you." I warned her.

"Okay, I have to get ready now." She said waiting for me to leave her room.

I sat on the couch in the living room and pretended to watch television.

"I'm heading out. See you tomorrow." Lexi called out to me as she left.

"See you later." I said back.

After 10 minutes, I was sure she was not coming back. So, I went into her bedroom and opened her laptop.

I was surprised she didn't have a passcode locking it as I was able to open her browser and go to the online social profile login page.

I used to break into DJ's account all the time when I

suspected him of cheating.

All I had to do was request a password reset. Most people's emails stay logged in on their laptops, so I was able to access her email without even logging in.

I opened the password reset email, followed the link, and reset her profile password.

After deleting the password reset email, I went directly to her profile messages.

Johnny messaged her a lot more than she revealed to me. I carefully read through their exchanges from tonight looking for any mention of me. I was suspicious she knew more about why Craig was ignoring me than she let on.

Johnny: Come over babe. Let's talk about it. I'm sorry you saw those pictures.

Lexi: I'm really hurt right now, Johnny. You ignored me all night to hook up with that girl. How could you sleep with her after she disrespected me that way at the restaurant? I'm glad Sam found those pictures.

Johnny: Look, I was drunk and hurt. I wasn't thinking clearly. And, Sam's groupie ass need to stay out of it! I am here to see you. You should be here, but every time I turn around Sam is here. No one invited her. She's jumping on all the band members. And, no one is even interested in her.

Lexi: Well, she has a right to be with them if she wants. But, I do find it odd that she was really into Luzar, and now all of a sudden, she's going after Craig.

Johnny: That's what groupies do. Anyway, I want to see you. Come up here and please don't bring Sam.

* * *

Lexi: Okay. Let me put some clothes on. See you soon.

My mouth was wide open in shock at what I read. I could not believe he called me a groupie that was jumping on all the band members.

I could not understand why Lexi did not tell me about this let alone defend me. I realized right there that Spring was right. Lexi was a two-faced bitch who was only looking out for herself.

I woke the next morning alert and my adrenaline pumping.

I hopped out the bed and went into the shower.

I blew out my long auburn hair, did my makeup, and wore a red wrap dress that fit me like a glove.

My phone rang and it was Spring.

"Hello, Sam. Are you ready for our reading today?" Spring said in her calm, therapeutic voice.

"Yes."

"Okay. Let's get the payment out of the way. I accept all major credit cards. The fee is $60 for 15 minutes."

I pulled out my wallet and read her the numbers on my credit card.

"You have a choice to make, Sam. They both really like you. You do not have to push so hard for their attention. There is nothing wrong with going after what you want, just learn to balance ambition and humility." Spring was giving me advice, but her riddled words went in one ear and out the other.

"But, will I have another chance with Craig?" I asked.

"You will, but you will have to travel to see him. The spirits are saying to go as a friend to him and build from there." Spring continued to advise.

"What about my roommate? Is she trying to sabotage me?"

"She's not trying to hurt you, nor is she trying to help you. She's a good friend, but she has her own path to worry about." Spring said.

"Why is it that she is having more success in her relationship than me?" I bombarded Spring with questions as I wanted to fit as many in my 15-minute reading as I could.

"Sometimes a person changes their energy and open themselves to receive love. People pick up each other's energy and respond accordingly. Sam, you need to focus on your own energy and become centered."

"How do I do that?" I demanded.

"Just open your mind. Try meditation and focus on your needs and who you are. Sam, you have everything you need to reach your goals. Trust yourself and follow your own path. Do not concern yourself with another's. Also, you need to keep your options open because there may be someone better coming towards you."

"Okay." I muttered under my breath.

"Well, we've reached our 15-minute mark. Everything is in place. Just allow it to happen. Enjoy the rest of your day." Spring hung up.

I was not satisfied with this reading.

16

"We should take a week off from work and fly to Los Angeles." I said to Lexi after ordering our drinks.

Lexi and I were experiencing an emptiness because the excitement of being with the band was fading. And, we were back to being ordinary.

I suggested we have drinks at a hip bar in East Atlanta Village.

I decided to hold in my anger at Lexi since she was still communicating with Johnny. I needed her to help me get back with Craig. It pained me that I had to be nice to her. But, I had to make sacrifices to get what I wanted.

"We should. I really miss Johnny. And, he did invite me to come out next month since they have some downtime in July."

"Find out the exact days and make sure Craig will be there. I'll find us some cheap plane tickets."

I thought about my reading with Spring. She said that I would reunite with Craig in Los Angeles and I had to make sure that happened.

After we caught a ride share back to the apartment, I

sat on the couch in the living room and immediately got onto my laptop to look for hotels in Los Angeles.

Lexi went into her room to message Johnny for the dates the band would have some downtime to hang out with us.

"He said the second week in July." Lexi called out from her bedroom.

I entered the dates and to my surprise found the perfect hotel on Sunset Boulevard and inexpensive airline tickets. I thought it must have been meant for me to go.

"Hey Lexi, I found where we are staying and some really inexpensive plane tickets." I called out.

Lexi walked out of her room and sat next to me on the couch.

"Let me see the hotel." She said peering down at my laptop.

"This place is really nice." She scrolled through the pictures of the boutique hotel.

"I'm going to do a bundle with the hotel, flight, and rental car. Maybe we can get a better discount that way." I said.

"Okay, well let me know what my half of everything is so I can tell Johnny."

"Why do you need to tell Johnny?" I asked.

"He's wiring me the money for the trip." She revealed.

"Oh, I didn't know that. Must be nice." I sneered.

"Is everything okay, Sam?" She looked at me startled at my response.

"Yeah, I'm sorry. It's just things aren't going the way I thought they would with Craig."

"Do you think it's because of what happened between you, him, and Luzar?"

She immediately tensed her face suggesting that she did not mean to reveal what she knew.

"What!?" I shouted out.

"I'm sorry, Sam. Johnny told me about the threesome." Lexi confessed, "I don't judge you for it. But, Craig may have an issue with it being his bandmate."

"What do you mean? Did Craig say this to Johnny?"

"Yeah, he did. Johnny made me promise not to say anything."

"Tell me everything he said!" I demanded. I could not believe she was hiding all of this information from me.

"Okay," Lexi cleared her throat, "Craig really liked you when we all first met last year. He was hurt that you were messaging Luzar and hooked up with him at the hotel. Craig asked Luzar to set up the threesome with you. That's why Craig came to the restaurant with us." Lexi paused and looked at me concerned if she should continue.

"What else, Lexi?"

"Do you really want to hear this?" Lexi asked with a concerned expression.

"Yes. I want to know everything." I crossed my arms over my chest bracing myself for what she had to say next.

"After the threesome, Craig said you seemed to prefer him over Luzar. So, he wanted to try again with you, but something happened the next day at a restaurant. He said you were behaving like a fame whore." Lexi tried to deliver this information gently, but it stung anyway.

"Fame whore!" I shouted, "Why would he think that?"

"He said you were more interested in the attention from his fans." She added.

I remembered how it felt when Craig's fans were ogling us on the street.

I was so wrapped up in being praised by these people, I did not realize how uncomfortable it made Craig.

116

I sat back on the couch.

"Why didn't you tell me this sooner?"

"I didn't know how. I didn't want to hurt your feelings."

"Well, now I'm hurt and embarrassed." I stood from the couch, grabbed my laptop, and stormed into my room, slamming the door behind me.

I sat on my bed, replaying everything Lexi revealed to me. I wondered if I should even go to Los Angeles.

17

Ding!

"You may now exit the plane. Thank you for flying with us. Enjoy your trip to Los Angeles." The flight attendant announced over the speaker.

I was so excited to be in Los Angeles. I thought about cancelling this trip, but Sophie encouraged me to take a risk and go after Craig.

Lexi and I did not speak most of the trip. I was still angry at her and embarrassed that she knew about my threesome with Craig and Luzar.

We walked directly to the shuttle stand to wait for the shuttle bus to take us to our rental car.

The sky was clear and blue with the afternoon sun shining brightly above. I put on my red designer shades.

I belonged here.

The shuttle bus pulled up and we climbed on carrying our luggage.

"I can't believe we're actually here!" Lexi gushed.

I gave her a strained smile then turned my back to her and stared out the window. I had no intention of hanging with her in Los Angeles. My only reason for being there with her was that she still had a connection with Johnny.

I realized I needed to play nice with Lexi until I got back with Craig. So, I turned back toward her and put on my most convincing fake smile.

"What do you think about this one?" I asked Lexi.

I modeled a red low-cut wrap top over a push-up bra with dark blue skinny jeans and strapped black heels.

I admired myself in the floor-length mirror. I looked like a runway model with my long slender body. My auburn hair had grown to my waist.

I felt beautiful.

"You look good." Lexi said as she applied her makeup while she sat on the bed.

The hotel room was a nice size with two full sized beds and a walk-in closet.

This night Lexi and I decided to get a drink at the hotel bar and explore the city.

I looked over at Lexi to see how she compared. She wore her dark brown hair down and parted in the middle. It came just past her shoulders. Her foundation made her brown skin bronzed.

She wore a black short skirt with a white crop top that tied in the front. She slipped on a pair of high heeled ankle boots. She paired her outfit with the designer purse Johnny bought her in Atlanta.

Lexi pulled out her phone and started texting.

"Are you texting Johnny?" I asked as I glanced at her phone.

"Yeah, Zach, the drummer from the band, has a side gig at a club tomorrow night. You wanna go?" She asked while she read Johnny's message on her phone.

"Sure, will Craig be there?"

"Yeah, he said everyone will be there to support Zach."

We made our way down to the hotel bar. It was small and dim. Only the bar area was lit with very soft lighting.

Almost every guy at the bar stared at us. Especially the bartender. He gave us free drinks and seemed very interested in Lexi.

He was attractive with dirty blond short hair and bright blue eyes that stood out with his tanned skin.

"So, how are you ladies enjoying L.A.?" He asked.

"The energy here is amazing." I said.

"It's the people," He said, "Everyone that moves here emits their hopes and dreams into the atmosphere."

"I like that." Lexi responded.

"I'm Brad." He said extending his hand out to Lexi.

"I'm Lexi and this is Sam."

"I get off in about 15 minutes if you guys want to hang out." Brad offered mostly to Lexi.

"Sure. That sound like fun." Lexi called out in a flirty tone.

Brad smiled shyly and walked away to wait on some other customers at the bar.

"Are you flirting with him?" I asked Lexi.

"Why not? He's cute." Lexi said mischievously.

"What about Johnny?"

"Johnny made it very clear that he was seeing other girls. So, I'm allowed to flirt." She took a sip of her drink and looked back at Brad.

Brad walked around the bar and greeted a tall blond guy with blue eyes. They almost looked like twins.

The guy walked towards me and Lexi.

"Hey, this is my friend Steve. He's from Sweden." Brad introduced his friend.

"This is Sam." Brad said as he pointed me out to Steve.

"Hey Sam." Steve said in a light accent.

He looked like a doll.

His skin did not have a pore in sight. And, his muscular body did not have an ounce of fat on it. He was perfect.

A little too perfect.

"So, you guys want to head back to my place?" Steve suggested, "I have a house in the Hollywood Hills that has an amazing view of the city."

"Yeah. His house is amazing!" Brad called out from behind the bar.

Lexi and I looked at each other. She shrugged her shoulders as if to say, 'Why not'.

"This view is amazing!" Lexi whispered to me.

Steve's home was modern. It was made mostly of concrete and glass. The windows in the living room covered the whole back wall which revealed an amazing view of the city below.

"I wonder what he does for a living." I whispered back to Lexi.

"Brad said he's a talent agent. And, that he works with a lot of big stars. He represents Brad also." Lexi said.

We left the huge glass wall and sat on a large grey L-shaped sofa that faced a white and grey marble fireplace with a large flat screen television above it.

Steve and Brad came into the living room with a glass of white wine in each hand. They handed Lexi and I a glass and sat next to us on the couch.

"So, how long have you lived here?" I asked Steve.

"Five years. I worked as an agent in Sweden then my company moved me out here. I bought this house around that same time. Are you thinking of moving to L.A.?"

"I've thought about it. It's so beautiful here." I said.

"You would definitely fit in here. You are extremely beautiful."

I blushed at his compliment.

I looked over at Lexi and Brad. They were sitting close to each other and Brad was whispering in her ear. They gave each other a knowing look, then Brad grabbed her hand and led her up the stairway.

I could not believe she went upstairs with him. What was she thinking. A part of me wanted to run up the stairs and drag her back down. But, I tried to keep my composure and just sat next to Steve on the couch.

"Your friend seems like a lot of fun." Steve said as he looked over my body seductively.

I started to feel uncomfortable. I was so upset with Lexi leaving me alone with Steve.

"Are you okay? You seem nervous." Steve asked with a concerned expression.

"I'm fine. Just not use to all of this." I said amazed at my honesty.

"I have something that can help you relax." Steve reached into his pocket and pulled out a small capsule with white powder inside.

"Oh, I don't do drugs." I blurted out, "I don't have an issue with anyone that does. It's just a personal preference."

I realized that I was rambling and immediately felt embarrassed.

"It is okay, Sam." Steve said with a strained smile.

"I love your southern accent." He tried to change the subject.

"I love your accent too." I said awkwardly.

We sat on the couch quietly for a long minute. Steve took the wine glass from my hand and sat it on a grey and white marble side table.

"Come here." He pulled me close and started kissing me.

His lips were so soft, and he smelled of expensive

cologne. I found him interesting, but his kiss did not feel right.

Also, he was not the one I came to see. I wanted to be with a rock star.

I was there to get another chance with Craig.

I pulled away from Steve.

"I'm sorry. I'm not really into this." I said to Steve.

He cleared his throat. I could see the pain of rejection on his face.

"Okay." He said trying to hide his disappointment, "Since your friend is staying with Brad, you can sleep in the guest room tonight. Follow me." He stood from the couch and walked quickly to the stairs.

I followed him.

When we reached the top of the stairs, I heard Lexi moaning. The door to their room was left slightly open enough that I could catch a glimpse of Lexi and Brad naked.

Lexi was sitting at the edge of the bed and Brad was on his knees before her with his head between her thighs.

I caught Steve peering into the room at them. He let out a sigh of disappointment.

"You can sleep here." He said coldly as he pointed to the room next to Lexi and Brad's.

"Thanks." I muttered, and I walked past Steve into the dark room.

Steve turned on the light and closed the door behind me. The room was white and small with a full-sized bed and grey night stand with a small grey lamp. Everything in the house was grey and white. So, boring.

I sat on the bed and replayed the night in my head. I was glad I said no to Steve's advances. Something about him reminded me of Luzar the first night I slept with him.

I took off my heels and decided to sleep in the bed fully

clothed, just to be safe.

Brad gave Lexi and I a ride back to our hotel the next day.

When we left, Steve never came out of his room. I was relieved, I did not want it to be more awkward.

Brad drove Steve's red convertible down the winding road. I sat in the back of the car while Brad and Lexi talked in the front.

I watched the palm trees and pedestrians walking by enjoying the bright, perfect day. Everything looked so picturesque and perfect. It felt surreal.

After Brad dropped us off, it was a little after 10 o'clock in the morning, so we decided to go out for breakfast. We drove our rental car to a restaurant in Santa Monica known for serving the best pancakes.

We didn't say much on the drive there. I was uncomfortable after seeing Lexi and Brad together in the bedroom last night. I wondered how she could be intimate with a stranger the night before she sees Johnny.

After the hostess sat Lexi and I at a small round table, we immediately looked through our menus, and tried to avoid eye contact.

"So, how did you like Steve?" Lexi asked trying to break our awkward silence.

"He was nice. But, I didn't feel a connection with him." I said, "You and Brad seemed to hit it off."

"Yeah, we did." Lexi responded avoiding my judgmental stare.

"So, are you going to see Brad again?"

"No. I don't plan on it." I could hear the annoyance in Lexi's voice.

"I guess you couldn't wait for Johnny, huh?"

"Maybe I can fuck Brad and Johnny at the same time. You seem to enjoy that type of thing." She snapped back at me.

We sat awkwardly quiet until the waitress came over and took our order.

After a few minutes of more silence, Lexi turned to me, "Sorry, I shouldn't have said that."

"It's fine. I'm sorry for bringing up Johnny."

"So, how are things going with you and Johnny?" I suspected they were having issues and wanted to make sure we were still going to the show.

"We're good. He said he'd leave us tickets at the door for the show tonight." She said.

"Did he say if Craig would be there?"

"Yeah, he said Craig will definitely be there."

18

The small venue on Sunset Boulevard for the drummer Zach's side band was packed.

I assumed they were mostly 'Death of Love' fans hoping to see the other band members.

It was difficult to see through the crowd in the barely lit room.

"Where are we supposed to meet them?" I asked Lexi who looked just as confused as I.

The venue was a lot smaller than it appeared on the outside. The stage was so small the drum set took up more than half of it.

The walls were covered in old torn flyers that had likely been there for decades. The only decent light was behind the bar. Since this was the best lit area, Lexi decided to stand here so Johnny could see us.

It worked because soon after Johnny pushed through the crowd towards us.

"Hey babe!" Johnny said excitedly as he pulled Lexi into his arms and kissed her.

Lexi stared into Johnny's eyes with infatuation and

smiled sweetly at something he whispered in her ear.

"Hey, Sam." Johnny said to me as if it were an afterthought.

He quickly turned his attention back to Lexi.

After we got our drinks from the bar, Johnny led Lexi and I through the crowd of fans to a small roped off lounge area by the tiny stage.

Everyone stared at us as we past by because we were with Johnny.

I liked the attention. It felt like being with the 'in' crowd and everyone wishing they were you.

The VIP lounge area had three small distressed couches. One side of the VIP was occupied by four women. Two were brunette and the other two were blond.

Johnny sat on the empty couch opposite the models and Lexi sat next to him. I sat at the end on the other side of Lexi.

I looked out into the crowd near the stage area to see if Craig was there. I became nervous that he may not show up.

"Is Craig here?" I whispered to Lexi.

"I'll ask Johnny." Lexi turned to Johnny.

Johnny leaned over Lexi's lap and looked right into my eyes, "Craig is standing in for the guitar player in Zach's band tonight."

Johnny looked at Lexi annoyed, stood up, and walked through a small door that lead to the backstage area.

I was pained by his reaction to me. I began to feel that it may have been a mistake for me to be there.

"Ignore him." Lexi said trying to make me feel better.

When Johnny came back out, one of the brunette models tried to get his attention by waving at him. He pretended to not see her and made his way back to his seat on the couch.

I could see the pain of rejection flash across her face even in the dark club. I could relate with her, I was not used to being rejected either.

"Hey, what's up?" I was startled by Craig's voice.

I looked up and he was standing over me. I did not notice him walk out of the backstage area.

"Hey." My heart started pounding with excitement as I stood to give Craig a hug.

"Glad you guys could make it to the show." He said returning my hug with a squeeze.

"Yeah. I was hoping to see you again." I blurted out. I could feel myself blush.

"Well, I'm glad to see you, Sam." Craig said with a laugh at my bashfulness.

"I have to go on stage. Let's hang out afterwards." Craig gave me another quick hug and walked back into the backstage area.

Lexi looked at me with a sweet smile at my moment with Craig.

My nervousness turned into excitement. I could not wait for the show to finish so that I could be with him.

The performance was not good.

After they finished their set, I could see several fans giving them fake praise for the bad performance.

After conversing with the fans, Craig made a bee-line straight to me. He seemed so happy to see me. The attention from him made my stomach flutter.

Before he could reach out to hug me, the other brunette model grabbed his arm and began gushing to him how she enjoyed the show. Craig glanced at me as she tried to occupy his attention.

He gave her a quick hug and thanked her for the compliment. Then, he turned back towards me.

"You looked so cool up there." I wanted to compliment

him without mentioning the bad performance of the band.

"Thanks. But, we sucked pretty bad up there." Craig said with a toothy grin.

The drummer, Zach, came into the VIP lounge, picked up one of the blond models and held her up in the air. While she giggled and squealed in excitement, he dropped her back onto the couch, straddled her, then roughly French kissed her.

Everyone could tell this made her uncomfortable. But, she let him have his way.

After his vulgar display of affection, Zach ran over to Craig.

"Where we going, dudes?" Zach yelled out.

Zach was obviously on some type of stimulate because he was way too hyper. This explained why his performance was so bad.

"I'm starving, man. We may hit up that after-hours diner." Craig said to Zach.

"Cool? We'll meet you dudes there?" Zach said in a fake surfer voice.

Zach walked away then turned around and held up his hand signaling the devil horns and stuck out his tongue. Then, he ran back to the blond model and started grabbing on her.

"He's really fucked up." Lexi whispered in my ear.

I was so glad to be out of that tiny, dark club and breathing the outside air.

The club was cool, but with the crowd it became stale and hard to breathe.

Johnny called a ride share for the four of us while Zach and his entourage of models rode in a separate SUV.

Craig sat in the front passenger seat and I sat by the

window next to Lexi and Johnny. Even with Craig in the car, I still felt like a third wheel in the back as Johnny and Lexi giggled and loved on each other.

This really upset me because Lexi was intimate with the hotel bartender just the night before. I wondered if Johnny would be so into her if he knew this.

We finally made it to the diner which was packed with people who looked as if they just left a nightclub. It was two o'clock in the morning and everyone seemed to be relieving their drunkenness with greasy food.

The diner was designed like the one's in movies from the 1950's with chrome and neon lights. The lights were bright on the inside making my eyes hurt from the adjustment from the night.

We found a booth in the back corner of the restaurant.

As we made our way to the available booth many of the patrons recognized Johnny and Craig. Once we sat down a waitress promptly came to our table.

After placing our orders, Johnny and Craig talked about the show for a few minutes while Lexi and I sat in awkward silence.

"So, how are you enjoying your trip?" Craig asked turning towards me.

"Good. Lexi and I went to a few places." I responded.

"Oh, really. Where did you go?" Craig asked.

"We went to the hotel bar and went to a famous pancake place." I said vaguely.

I decided not to mention Steve and Brad from the night before. Even though I did not have sex with Steve, Craig may not have liked that we went to a stranger's house in the Hollywood Hills.

"I can show you around tomorrow. There are some cool places you'll like." Craig said giving me a wink.

He was making future plans with me. I knew this was

a sign that he was serious about me. Then my moment was interrupted when Zach yelled at us from across the diner.

"There's nowhere to sit!" Zach yelled out.

He was accompanied by the same four models from the club.

Many of the patrons ignored him.

"Johnny, Craig! How y'all dickheads get the last booth." Zach said loudly as he and the four models approached us.

Zach and his models stood over us. The brunette stared puzzled at Johnny and Lexi.

"Hey, Johnny." The brunette model said in a soft, sweet voice.

"What's up?" Johnny responded looking up pretending he did not know she was standing there the whole time.

"We're just hanging out. I text you this morning." She glanced at Lexi.

I thought Lexi would be upset, but she surprisingly kept her cool.

"Well, I'm glad you and your friends enjoyed Zach's show." Johnny said and then turned his attention back to Lexi.

The booth behind us became available so Zach shoved the blond he was with to sit at the table cornering her by the wall. The other three models squeezed into the booth seat across from him.

Craig and Johnny rolled their eyes in disapproval.

It impressed me that Craig did not show interest in Zach's girls. He was not a stereotypical rock star. Which made him even more interesting.

Lexi and Johnny left the diner together in a ride share. Zach and his models followed Craig and I into the parking lot.

While Craig was requesting a ride share for he and I, Zach came up behind me and wrapped his arms around my waist.

"So, I hear you like to get gang banged." Zach whispered in my ear, "I got some of the purest white powder and we can all have a party."

I struggled away from Zach's grasp and stood close to Craig, who did not notice what happened from staring at the ride share app on his phone.

Zach laughed at me.

A black SUV pulled up and Zach climbed in with his models. I was relieved he was gone, leaving me alone in the parking lot with Craig.

19

I sat on a couch in Craig's living room staring out at the sun lit beach through the tall glass sliding doors. I came back to Craig's home last night in Venice Beach.

He had a three-story modern style block home on the beach in a secluded neighborhood. The back of his house was mostly glass, so the sunlight filled the home and each room had a view of the beach.

I day dreamed about us making love last night to the sound of the ocean waves.

He left the balcony door to his bedroom open all night so that the smell of the ocean filled the room. I imagined myself living here with him.

I continued to stare out at the beach sitting cross-legged in one of Craig's t-shirts.

I felt at peace, like I was finally home. I thought to myself that I never wanted to leave.

Craig was in the kitchen behind me cooking breakfast.

"It smells really good in there." I turned around on the couch to watch him scramble eggs at the stove.

"It'll taste even better." He said winking at me.

* * *

After breakfast, we walked on the beach.

There was only one other couple outside, so it felt as if we had the whole beach to ourselves.

Craig wore a pair of blue swimming trunks and I just had on the large white t-shirt that barely covered my bare butt.

We held hands and walked along the beach in the morning sunlight as a light breeze from the ocean kept us cool.

"I'm glad you're here." Craig said looking into my eyes.

"I'm happy to be here as well."

"Did you come out here to L.A. to see me?"

"Yes. I was concerned with the way we left things when you were in Atlanta. I'm sorry if I did anything to hurt you. I really like you Craig."

Craig turned me around to face him.

"I have to be honest with you." He said, "It bothered me that you went after Luzar when I made it clear that I wanted you. You sort of behaved like all the other girls that he passes around. When I took you to breakfast that time, you seemed more interested in the attention from my fans than you were with me."

I was taken aback by his honesty.

"Craig, you have to understand that this is all new to me. I'm not used to the attention. And, with Luzar, I met him first backstage at the show last year. It had nothing to do with preference. I was getting to know you both at the same time. But, now I know how I feel. When the three of us were intimate, I felt closer to you. After that, Luzar did not matter anymore."

Everything I said to Craig was true. Luzar was not who I wanted anymore. I rarely thought about him. I was falling in love with Craig, and I knew he was falling in love with me too.

20

I spent the rest of my time in Los Angeles with Craig.

I assumed Lexi was with Johnny because I did not see her until the day of our flight back to Atlanta.

Lexi and I barely spoke on the plane.

We were both reminiscing about the past few days.

Craig took me to some amazing places.

On my last night, he surprised me with a beautiful gold necklace with a 2-carat diamond cluster pendent in the shape of a heart.

This was the first time anyone had given me something so luxurious.

Back in Atlanta, Lexi and I were still barely speaking. I realized that I did not need her anymore. And, her sleeping around and cheating on Johnny in Los Angeles was something I wanted no part of. I did not want Craig to see me as a cheater like her, so I had to distance myself.

I could not wait to call Sophie to tell her all about my time with Craig. I dialed her number and she answered on the first ring.

"Where have you been, Miss Hollywood? I've been

calling you for days! Tell me everything that happened while you were out there." Sophie said excitedly over the phone.

I told her about my time staying with Craig. And, sent her a picture of the necklace he bought for me. Then, I told her about the first night and Lexi sleeping with the bartender.

"You should tell Craig about her cheating on Johnny." Sophie said, "You don't want him to find out and wonder why you didn't say anything. And, you need to stay away from her."

"You're right, Sophie. She's just a groupie and I can't risk my relationship with Craig by being loyal to her." I said.

I decided I would confess everything that happened the first night in Los Angeles to Craig.

Later that day, Craig messaged me a picture of the view from his balcony of the beach. I decided to send him a message.

Sam: I miss you.

I saw that he read the message a few moments later.

Craig: I miss you more. How's it going?

Sam: I'm okay. There's something I have to tell you about the first night Lexi and I were in L.A.

Craig: Okay? What happened?

I type out everything in detail about how we met the bartender and his friend, staying at the guys Hollywood Hills home, and Lexi being with the bartender.

Craig read the long message. After about five minutes,

he responded.

Craig: That's between Johnny and Lexi. I really don't want to be in the middle of their drama. They seem to enjoy each other. And, why would you go to some strange guy's house that you met for like 5 minutes?

His bluntness in the message shocked me. I did not expect him to react like this. Then, I realized that I made a mistake revealing that night to him.

Sam: I just don't want you to think that I'm like her.

Craig: Why would you worry about being like Lexi? She seems like a really good friend to you. And, Johnny really likes her. Let's just focus on us. I don't need to know Johnny and Lexi's business. I'm going out. Talk to you later.

I thought he would be more appreciative with my honesty.

I sat on my bed staring at my laptop, praying that I did not make a mistake telling him this.

"Why are you telling my business to Craig?!" Lexi yelled at me in the break room of the department store.

"My business is not yours to tell!" She continued to shout.

Lexi was so loud, one of the associates walked in to see what the commotion was about.

"Look, I'm with Craig now and I can't keep secrets from him." I said trying to keep my composure.

"What?! You think sleeping with him for a few days makes you a couple? Girl, wake up!" Lexi said crossing her arms.

"Craig and I are on a different level than you and Johnny."

"Oh, really! What level are you and Luzar on? Because you seem to be bouncing your way through the whole band!"

She stormed out of the break room leaving me alone with a few of the sales associates standing nearby staring at me in shock.

Lexi and I avoided each other for a week after our argument.

Every time I messaged Craig, he just replied that he was busy and would message me another time.

I should have known that Craig would have become jealous of me going to another man's home. I was too consumed with Lexi's behavior that night, I did not realize that Craig would be hurt by my actions as well.

I decided to log into my fake social profile to look through his profile pictures. I also went through his friends' profile pictures and any tags on his name.

While I snooped through the profiles, I received a notification that Luzar sent me a private message on my real profile.

I decided to wait before opening it, I did not want him to see that I read it.

Although I was falling in love with Craig, I still got butterflies in my stomach at the thought of Luzar messaging me.

My phone chimed. It was a text from Sophie.

Sophie: DJ's been a mess since you left. He's been high and wasted almost every night at the bar. He also got into an altercation with his boss and lost his job. He's been really behind on the mortgage payments and may be

losing the house. You should call him.

Sam: I'll give DJ a call later.

I knew he was heartbroken by my leaving, but I did not imagine that it was this bad. But, I was dealing with my own problems with Craig's aloofness.

I saw that 32 minutes went by and realized it was a good time to open Luzar's message.

Luzar: Hey, Sam. I heard you came to LA. Now, why didn't you call me? I'd loved to have spent some time with you. I thought we had fun together when I was in Atlanta. Well, we start our tour soon and the band will be in the ATL in a few months. I'd like to see you again. Kiss

Maybe I can just be friendly. I mean Spring said to be his friend. I tried to justify wanting to reply to him.

Craig had not mentioned to me that he would be here with the band in a few months.

This made me question whether he was into me. I thought that if Craig wanted to ignore me, why could I not be friends with him.

Sam: Sorry, I didn't get a chance to hang out with you. I look forward to seeing you guys when you're in Atlanta.

Short and simple. That seemed like a message a friend would send.

I received a reply from Luzar immediately.

Luzar: You're a beautiful woman, Sam. I really need to see you again. I can't get you out of my head.

* * *

I was shocked reading his message. I did not expect this from him. Especially, after the way he treated me.

I realized that I needed to be careful. I was still attracted to him, but I did love Craig and did not want to lose him again.

Sam: Thank you. I have gotten closer with Craig, so you and I will have to hang out as friends.

I nervously waited for his to reply.

Luzar: We'll be best friends.

I could not deny the giddiness I felt reading his response. This was bad.

I began to feel as if I were betraying Craig with my feelings stirring up again for Luzar.

But, I was still confused why Craig wasn't the one telling me about the upcoming show.

Sam: Craig, why didn't you tell me about the band's tour and coming to Atlanta in a few months?

I did not expect Craig to message me back for a while, so I closed my laptop and watched television.

The message notification dinged on my laptop. I ran into my room and opened it to see that Craig responded.

Craig: How did you know about the tour dates? It hasn't been confirmed yet. I was waiting for the confirmation of the new dates before telling you.

Sam: Luzar just sent me a message about it. I was wondering why you didn't tell me?

Craig read the message almost as soon as I hit send. My heart was racing. Why did I have to say something? Luzar was always a sore spot for Craig.

I rested my head in my hands wondering why I continued to make these stupid mistakes that sabotaged my chances with Craig.

Craig: Like I said, I was waiting for the new dates to be confirmed. So, you're still going after Luzar I see. Have a nice life, Sam.

All the air escaped my mouth as my chest caved in from reading Craig's response. My heart pounded so hard in my chest, it became sore with each beat.

With my hands trembling, I quickly started typing a reply to Craig to try and salvage the situation.

Sam: I'm not chasing Luzar. He messaged me. I told him you and I were getting close. It just bothered me that he was telling me about the tour dates and not you.

Craig read the message. I waited, expecting him to reply, but he never did.

"Sam are you crazy!" Sophie scolded me as I sat crying on the living room couch, "You should have ignored Luzar's message! Especially after the way he treated you."

I called Sophie crying hysterically and begged her to come over.

We sat on the couch and I showed her the messages.

"But, I didn't say anything sexual to Luzar." I spit out between my tears.

"It doesn't matter, Sam. You never should have

responded." Sophie continued to scold me.

"What do you think I should do? I have to make this right, Sophie."

"Sam, you fucked up royally. You may not be able to fix it this time."

Sophie's response angered me. Who did she think she was?

"Oh, what do you know, Sophie? What rock stars have you dated? Better yet, what human has ever been interested in you?"

Sophie's face became red and her eyes widened with fury.

I never saw her so angry and I soon began to regret my words.

"Sam, you are a self-absorbed groupie who'd fuck anybody to be in the rock scene. Craig is ditching you because he finally sees the trash that you really are."

Sophie stood over me as I sat back on the couch afraid for what she may say next. She began to tremble as she pursed her lips.

"If you were a real friend to me, Sam. And, cared to ask about my life, you'd notice the diamond ring on my finger."

She held up her hand revealing gold ring with a small diamond on top.

"I'm engaged. So, I guess there is at least one human who is interested in me."

Sophie grabbed her purse and stormed out of the apartment.

I sat still on the couch staring at the door Sophie stormed out of.

I could not believe she was getting married. I never thought she would get married before me.

I went into my room and laid on my bed trying to figure out how to rectify my situation with Craig.

I was upset with myself for saying those harsh things to Sophie. But, her and I had fallen out before and I knew she would forgive me.

Lexi came into the apartment from work. I decided to try and talk to her.

I knocked on her bedroom door.

"What's up?" She called out.

I opened the door to find her sitting on the bed crossed-legged in a long red cotton dress with her laptop opened on her lap.

"Hey, I just wanted to talk to you." I said cautiously entering her room and sitting on the bed.

"Okay?" She was slightly annoyed.

I needed to tread carefully. I was not sure if she was still upset with me.

"I want to apologize for what happened. I shouldn't have said anything to Craig about our first night in LA. I didn't mean for it to get back to Johnny."

"They're bandmates and friends, Sam. You didn't think he would say anything to Johnny."

"Well, I thought we could go out for a drink in Midtown tonight. My treat." I suggested.

"I'm really tired, Sam. Let's do that another time." She looked down and focused her attention onto her laptop.

"Okay."

I didn't know what else to say. So, I walked out of her room and she started typing.

21

A month went by and Lexi, Sophie, nor Craig were communicating with me. I was a zombie at work. I could barely concentrate and barely made my sales quota that month.

I tried several times to get back in Lexi's good graces, but she was not having it.

I was finally able to reconcile with Sophie and I was grateful, but I needed Lexi if I had yet another shot at Craig.

It was a few more weeks before the band would perform in Atlanta. I had to figure out something fast.

I had just gotten off work and set in my car in the mall's garage.

I could not believe I was back in this position again.

I wished I could take everything back and start over.

I had Craig from the beginning. All I had to do was just be with him and ignore everything else.

But, wishing could not help me at this point.

Back at the apartment, I sat on Lexi's bed and used the

forgot password link to send to her email and change the password.

Once I was in her profile, I went directly to her private messages. And, just as I guessed, her and Johnny were still in communication. There was an unread message from Johnny.

I thought 'What the hell' and opened the message.

Johnny: Lexi, I really want to see you at the show. We're both in the wrong. I DO like you. I'll leave you a backstage pass at the ticket window. But, don't bring Sam. Craig doesn't want to see her.

I could not let Lexi go to the concert without me.

She would leave me behind and I could not bear the thought of her living the life I knew I was destined for.

I decided to delete the message from Johnny. I felt bad for doing this, but I needed to be at that show.

I realized that deleting the message Lexi may not go to the show. So, I needed to find a way to convince her to go with me.

Then, I remembered Luzar inviting me.

I decided to message him and see if he would give me two passes for the show. That way I could bring Lexi with me, and if she goes backstage I could go back with her.

I had no intention of hooking up with Luzar again. But, I was willing to use him to get another chance with Craig.

It took a few hours for Luzar to respond to my message about the passes.

I nervously paced around the apartment and checked my profile notifications constantly to see if he responded.

When he finally replied I was about to give up hope.

Luzar: Of course I'll give you passes. I can't give all

access, but you'll be able to see us after the show. I'll leave them at will call.

I let out a sigh of relief. It was not all access, but it was something I could work with. All I had to do was convince Lexi to go with me.

I watched a movie in the living room while I waited for Lexi to come home from work. My plan had to work. But, Lexi and I had been so distant, I was not sure if she would even talk to me.

Lexi walked into the apartment. She looked at me, and then walked directly to her room.

I decided to wait a few minutes before going into her room.

She left her bedroom door open, so I stood in the doorway.

Lexi was sitting on her bed starring angrily at her laptop.

"Hey, is everything okay?" I stepped through the doorway cautiously.

"My password isn't working for my profile." She said as she continued to type in the code on her laptop.

"You may have to reset it." I said.

"Yeah, that's what I'm doing now."

I proceeded further into her room.

"Luzar sent me a message saying he left two tickets to the concert. I was wondering if you wanted to go with me."

Lexi looked up at me with a puzzled expression.

"I don't know if I want to go." She said.

"Lexi, I know you really like Johnny. Don't message him. Just wait until the day of the show and we can go together. You have to at least give it one more shot." I sat on the edge of her bed.

Lexi let out a deep sigh as she contemplated going to the concert with me.

"Okay, I'll think about it."

"Don't contact him. Give him some time to miss you."

I had to be sure she did not message him and find out about the all access pass he left for her. More important, I had to make sure she did not go without me.

22

The next few weeks went by quickly and it was the day of the show.

Lexi decided to drive us to the concert.

She parked in the lot across from the venue which was an old renovated cathedral.

I got our tickets and after show passes from will call.

Luzar gave us tickets for general admission, so we to find a spot on the floor to the left of the stage to stand.

It was the perfect spot with a clear view of the stage. This way Craig had a clear view of me as well.

The opening band was from Paris and they were really good. I made eye contact with the singer a few times and he smiled at me.

Finally, after an intermission, the lights dimmed indicating that 'Death of Love' was about to perform. The crowd started clapping and cheering. And, a wave of excitement rushed through me as I watched the band walk onto the stage.

They began playing with everyone dancing and singing energetically.

I stood slightly in front of Lexi so that Craig could see me.

He glanced at me a few times throughout the show. Luzar was too into the crowd being into him so he didn't pay attention to anyone.

Johnny, looked directly at Lexi with a hurt expression.

Lexi was hard to read. She just stared back at Johnny with a blank expression throughout their performance.

The show was amazing as expected.

Lexi and I made our way down the stairs to the after show area being held in a large empty space with a small stage and a bar on either side.

There were about 50 people there, mostly attractive girls.

It was reminiscent of the night I met the band.

Lexi and I sat on the edge of the small stage. I looked around and spotted the three women that were with Luzar at the hotel when the band first came to Atlanta.

One of the women noticed us and whispered to the other two. They looked back at us and rolled their eyes.

"So, are you here for Luzar or Craig?" Lexi asked.

"Are you going to hook up with Johnny?" I snapped back at her.

"I don't know." She said dismissively, "Maybe I should leave."

Lexi climbed down from the stage.

As soon as she planted her feet on the floor, Johnny walked out from the backstage area.

Their eyes connected, and he began walking towards her, but a girl with long dark hair grabbed his arm and started hugging him. But, he never took his eyes off Lexi as she stood still staring back at him.

Johnny pulled away from the girl's grasp thanked her for coming to the show and walked to Lexi. He had a big smile on his face as he embraced her in a hug.

They exchanged a few words, then she came back to the stage and sat next to me.

Her whole mood changed after that moment.

A few moments later, Craig walked out.

He walked past Lexi and I straight to the girls standing with Luzar. They all gave him a hug and talked excitedly with him.

I sat frozen next to Lexi.

"Should I go over there?" I turned to Lexi.

"Why not? He's the one you came to see right?"

I took a deep breath and climbed off the edge of the small stage.

My knees trembled as I walked across the large room to Craig.

I tapped his shoulder and he turned around.

"Hey, how are you?"

I stared into his eyes and they were cold.

"Good, how are you?" His voice was flat with no emotion.

"I'm good."

He stared blankly at me.

I didn't know what to say next. So, I stood there hoping he would.

"Well, it's good to see you again, Sam. I hope you enjoyed the show."

He gave me a hug, then held up his hand dismissively saying goodbye.

I saw the women snickering amongst each other at my expense.

I awkwardly walked back to the stage. It seemed like the longest walk of shame.

Lexi sat on the edge of the stage staring at me mortified at the way Craig dismissed me.

I climbed onto the stage and tried my best to keep my composure.

"Johnny told me they're having an afterparty at a bar in Atlantic Station." Lexi said, "Maybe you can try to talk with Craig again."

"He was so cold to me Lexi." I couldn't take my eyes off him.

"What do you want to do?" Lexi asked concerned.

"I don't know."

"Well, it's worth a shot, Sam. Craig's already done his worse."

Lexi and I walked into a packed upscale bar in Atlantic Station.

It was a small bar with plush chairs tucked in the corners and a long bar with almost every brand of liquor available that sat in a lit case.

Lexi spotted Johnny and Zach talking to some women at the bar.

Most of the women standing around were hoping for a chance to date a rock star. And, a few guys hung around hoping to score with the unlucky ones that were rejected.

As we made our way through the crowd, I looked frantically for Craig. But, I did not see any sign of him.

Johnny hugged Lexi and glanced annoyingly at me.

"Hey, Sam." He said condescendingly.

I did not respond. I just continued scanning the room.

Zach stood at the bar and stared at me with a smirk on his face. He looked as if he knew an inside joke about me, which made me feel uneasy.

Johnny bought Lexi and I a drink.

While I quietly sipped my cocktail, the lead singer from the opening band walked over. He was young at 21 years with a baby face and bright blue eyes. His hair was dyed black and gelled into small spikes all over. He was really tall, about 6'3 and slim.

I overheard him say something to Johnny.

He looked at me, then leaned over toward me.

"Hello, how are you?" He said in a thick French accent.

"I'm good, how are you?" I answered back.

"Fine. I am Fred." He reached out his long thin hand to me.

I shook his hand.

"I'm Sam."

"I saw you at the show. You are very beautiful, Sam." He said smiling widely to reveal his cigarette stained teeth.

"Thanks. You were amazing on stage. I loved your show." I blushed as he stared into my eyes.

It was nice to hear a complement after being rejected by Craig.

I would have welcomed the attention from Fred, but tonight I was on a mission to find Craig.

Luckily, Zach, who was intoxicated, started talking nonsense to Fred and Johnny. So, I took this opportunity to pull Lexi to the side.

"Ask Johnny if Craig is coming." I whispered to her.

Lexi nodded and walked to Johnny and quietly asked whispered to him.

Johnny shook his head no. Lexi looked at me with a sorrowful expression.

My heart sank.

Lexi walked back to me.

"He said Craig and Luzar went somewhere else. And, he's not sure where."

Not willing to give up hope I decided to text him.

Sam: Hey, Lexi and I are at this bar in Atlantic Station. Are you coming by? Maybe we can come to where you

are.

After a minute went by, he replied.

Craig: Sorry, I'm too busy reading a long book.

My whole body began to shake and Lexi saw that I was about to have a nervous breakdown. She whispered something to Johnny and quickly pulled me outside.

We walked quickly to the metered parking.

As soon as we got into the car, I let out all the tears and frustration.

I cried hysterically the whole drive back to the apartment.

When we pulled up to the front of our building, I was weak and exhausted. Lexi had to help me out of the car and walk me inside.

I sat on the couch in a state of disbelief.

Craig was a different person from the man I fell in love with in Los Angeles.

Lexi handed me a glass of wine.

"Sam, are you going to be okay?"

"I'll be okay. I just..." The tears welled in my eyes again and I had to catch my breath.

I couldn't believe this was happening to me.

Lexi's cellphone chimed. It must have been Johnny texting her to come back.

She checked her phone.

"I have to go back. Is there anything you need?" Lexi sat down next to me and tried to console me.

"I'm fine, Lexi. Go ahead."

She went into her room to pack an overnight bag.

As I sat on the couch, my blood felt as if it were boiling and I threw the wine glass, smashing it into pieces on the floor.

"Sam, what happened?" Lexi yelled as she ran from her room.

"It slipped out of my hand." I said trying to contain my rage.

Looking at Lexi, I became angrier.

"This was supposed to be my destiny. I am the one who should be dating a rock star, not you. This is my dream. You don't even want it." I rubbed my cheeks continuous causing the tears that streamed down my face to sting.

I don't know what came over me, but I stood up and began breathing heavily.

"You were supposed to help me!!" I shouted at Lexi.

Her expression became bewildered as she held up her hands and slowly stepped back.

"Sam, what is wrong with you? What the hell are you talking about?" Lexi said grabbing her overnight bag from the floor.

I didn't respond. I just stood in front of her enraged.

"I'm leaving. Try to get some rest, Sam."

Lexi walked out, leaving me standing in the middle of the living room, alone.

23

"I only have a 3:00 pm slot open for a 15-minute reading." Spring said over the phone.

I called Spring as soon as I awoke the next morning and begged her to fit me in for a reading.

"Okay, I can do that. Thanks, Spring." I said, my voice hoarse from crying all night.

I knew Spring could tell something was wrong from the careful way she spoke to me.

Sophie called my cellphone all morning, but I really didn't feel like talking to her.

I was supposed to be with Craig. Instead, I just sat on my bed staring out my window.

I was so exhausted from crying all last night, I did not have any energy left to cry anymore.

I realized it was over.

I could not place at what point I made a mistake. I felt so many different emotions, I could not focus on one thought. All I could do was sit on my bed and stare out the window.

* * *

It was finally 2:45 pm. The time seemed to move slowly.

My stomach grumbled, but I was too depressed to eat anything.

I spent the whole morning napping, watching television, and cyber stalking the Craig.

I waited by my cellphone anticipating Spring's call.

I needed to know why things did not work out last night. And, if it was completely over.

My phone rang and I quickly answered.

Spring gave her usual greeting then asked for my credit card number for payment.

After giving her my credit card number, she became unusually quiet.

"Sam. I'm having trouble with your credit card. It's declined." Spring said.

"What? It should work." I said shocked.

"I tried it twice. Do you have another card we can try?"

"Sure."

I pulled my bank card out of my wallet and read the numbers to her. I did not want to use this card because I had rent due next week and would be short.

But, this reading was more important.

"Okay, that one went through. Let's get started."

I explained everything that happened.

From visiting Craig in Los Angeles up to last night, including breaking into Lexi's online social profile.

"First, Sam, I never meant to imply that Lexi was your enemy in any way. It is never wise to invade someone's privacy." She sighed loudly, "What I meant was that she could assist you in reaching your goals, which it sounds like she did. But, she has her own destiny that she will pursue even if it means leaving you behind. All you had to do was be a friend to everyone and the universe would have handled the rest."

Spring cleared her throat.

"You cannot interfere with another's path because no matter what, the path will continue. You need to focus on what is happening on your own path. You need to take care of yourself, first. Be more attentive to the changes in your life or you will miss out on amazing opportunities. You need to keep your options open because there will be others who will pursue you. Do you understand what I'm saying, Sam?"

"I understand." I said disappointed.

"Well, that is all the time I have, Sam. Take care of yourself. Goodbye."

After saying aloud everything that I did this past year, I felt ashamed.

I checked my phone and saw that Sophie sent me several text messages. I read the last one she sent.

Sophie: You need to call me. DJ may be losing the house to foreclosure.

"Well, that explains why my credit card was declined." I said to Sophie over the phone.

My name was still on the mortgage and DJ stopped paying it a few months ago. This affected my credit and the credit card company closed my account.

"You need to call him, Sam. He's a mess." Sophie said.

I was startled when Lexi barged into my room.

"I need to talk to you when you're off the phone." Her face was tense as she turned away and stormed into the living room.

"Hey, Sophie let me call you back later."

I hung up with Sophie and walked into the living room where Lexi was sitting on the couch with her mouth turned upward.

"What's up?" I said cautiously.

"Sam, have you been breaking into my account and deleting my messages?"

"What do you mean?" I pretended to be confused.

"Johnny said he sent me a private message that he left an all access pass for me at will call. He also showed me that the message indicated I read it, which is not likely because I did not. Sam, did you break into my account and delete the message?"

"Why would I do that?" I tried to sound convincing.

"Sam, that was the second time my password did not work. I know you went on my laptop and changed my password."

Lexi stood from the couch and walked towards me. She stopped about a foot from my face.

"Sam, you are a manipulative, sad person. This is why Craig nor Luzar want you. They saw right through you."

She turn away and walked to her bedroom.

After my confrontation with Lexi, I decided it was time to call DJ and figure out what to do about the house.

"Hey, Sam!" DJ sounded different on the phone. He sounded like he had been drinking.

"DJ, what's going on? I spoke to Sophie. Is the house really going into foreclosure?"

"Well, I'm filing for bankruptcy and the house will likely be safe. It's been rough since you left, Sam."

A part of me still cared for DJ. Hearing the sadness in his voice made me hurt. He was a good man and he did not deserve to go through this.

"My credit card was declined today, so I assume it was cancelled because of the mortgage." I said.

"Sam, I'm sorry. I didn't want you to be harmed due to my messiness. I'll do whatever it takes to fix it. I got a job at a home improvement retail store, so I'll be able to make up the payments."

It was so heartbreaking to hear him sound so defeated.

"Sam, let me come up there and take you out for dinner. I miss you."

I knew DJ didn't have a lot of money, so I decided to cook for him at the apartment while Lexi was at her friends place.

He looked the same, but was quiet and sad.

He needed someone to love him.

After eating we sat on the couch and talked.

"DJ, I honestly thought you would have met someone else and moved on."

I really wished he had met someone else and moved on. I did not feel the same love for him as I once did a long time ago.

"I did date someone for a few months. But, she's not you, Sam."

When he said he dated someone else, it surprisingly made me jealous.

After everything I went through with Luzar and Craig, it felt good to be wanted.

He leaned in and kissed me.

And, I returned his kiss.

It's been so long since I kissed him that it felt as if I were kissing someone new.

He pulled me up from the couch and lead me into my bedroom.

I stood frozen as I watched him remove his clothes. He stood in front of me completely naked and I glanced over his familiar body.

He pulled my dress to the floor and guided me to the bed.

"I love you." He whispered.

Lexi and I stayed cordial to one another the remainder of our lease on the apartment. I knew our friendship was dead, so I did not push to reconcile.

DJ cut back on his drinking and drug use and he was able to save the house from foreclosure through bankruptcy.

After my experience living in the city, it was strange moving back to Fayetteville.

The open fields and small town was calming, but I missed the excitement of living in Atlanta.

Occasionally, Sophie and I would go into midtown for dinner and drinks.

I quit my job at the department store and got a job at a high-end spa in a luxury hotel.

I occasionally looked on Lexi's profile page with my fake account.

She quit the department store as well and moved in with Johnny in Los Angeles.

As I looked through Lexi's pictures on her profile, I decided to check Craig's profile and looked through his pictures.

Craig did not have many pictures, so I could not tell if he had a girlfriend or not.

Luzar was still with his model girlfriend. He finally put pictures of her on his profile. I surprisingly was not upset. It did not phase me at all.

I switched back to my real page.

I hadn't added anything to my profile in a while. I decided it was best to stay off there and try to move on.

I noticed a notification in my inbox.

It was a new private message.

I opened it and recognized the tall French lead singer

from the opening band from the show.

I remembered how he tried to talk to me at the after party in Atlantic Station.

Fred: Hello, beautiful. It took me a long time to find you. I wanted to get to know you better. Is that okay? My band will be performing in Atlanta soon. Will you come?

I became excited and intrigued at the message.

As I sat at my computer deciding how to reply, I began to fantasize about living in Paris.

The End

Read the complete series:

Star Reacher

Among the Stars

Dust from Stars